WEIRD WILD WEST

PART 3 - THE FREAKS OF MOJO COUNTY

CARTER RYDYR AND ETHAN SOMERVILLE

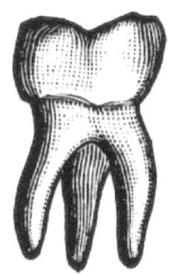

Copyright 2019 © Carter Rydyr & Ethan Somerville

Based on the comic story, *The Spazmos of Mojo County*, by Antoinette Rydyr and Steve Carter
Copyright © 1994

All rights reserved. No part of this book may be used or reproduced by any means, graphic, electronic, or mechanical, including photocopying, recording, taping or by any information storage retrieval system without the written permission of the publisher except in the case of brief quotations embodied in critical articles and reviews.

This is a work of fiction. All of the characters, names, incidents, organizations, and dialogue in this novel are either the products of the author's imagination or are used fictitiously.

JournalStone/Bizarro Pulp Press books may be ordered through booksellers or by contacting:
JournalStone
www.journalstone.com

The views expressed in this work are solely those of the authors and do not necessarily reflect the views of the publisher, and the publisher hereby disclaims any responsibility for them.

ISBN: 978-1-947654-95-2 (sc)
ISBN: 978-1-947654-96-9 (ebook)

Bizarro Pulp Press rev. date: June 7, 2019

Printed in the United States of America

Cover Art & Design; Interior Illustrations:: SCAR – Steve Carter and Antoinette Rydyr
Interior Layout: Jess Landry

Edited by Scarlett R. Algee
Proofread by Sean Leonard

PART 3 - THE FREAKS OF MOJO COUNTY

CHAPTER 1

Where the Kentessee Woods ran down from the Dragonback Mountain range, into lower foothills filled with all manner of bizarre creatures, lay the backwater province known as Mojo County. Its capital had been named Mojohoke after some long-forgotten indian chief, but it was now known simply as Mojo Town. The only reason this wide place in the road had even developed was because back in the dim and distant past, a meteorite had struck and scorched enough forest for people—fleeing the forest's many ravenous predators—to emerge and start cultivating the land.

Mojo Town started as a ramshackle collection of shanties and saloons, but when the mule trains started using it as a way station between Bhigge Smoche and the mines in the west, it developed into a thriving town. The rednecks, the moonshiners, and the hillbillies were all forced to move to the fringes, near the big hill at the back of town that had been created when the meteorite hit.

At the very top of the hill stood the remains of the Mojo County Orphanage, with the county junkyard on one side and the cemetery on the other. One road, known as Boneyard Way, led to all three. Townsfolk who travelled up that road could either turn off at the cemetery or the junkyard.

But even when the orphanage had been in use, the locals paid it very little mind, remaining unconcerned about its occupants, so long as the little unwanted brats kept quiet and didn't cause any trouble. No one had ever figured out what was *really* going on up there.

The ghostly building still dominated the hill behind the cemetery, now surrounded by weeds and thorns, burnt out and crumbling. A tall wall separated the orphanage and the junkyard, and between the orphanage and the children's cemetery ran an iron fence with a rusty gate. Both barriers were festooned with faded *Keep Out* signs, but broken through in several places by local children who wanted to explore—and who invariably raced out screaming only a few minutes later. Since there was a dispute over the ownership of the old place, it continued to cast its long, creepy shadow over the graveyard.

Although recent attempts had been made to beautify Mojo County Cemetery by cultivating healthy trees and cheerful flowering plants, poisons in the soil had stunted and twisted the growths into far more appropriate forms. Now the gnarled trees stretched witch-fingers across the gravelled paths, tangling up with others across the way, and long vines straggled everywhere. Pus-yellow and bile-green mosses and lichens grew all over the graves, and what flowers did manage to sprout were small and insipid, and invariably stank of the corpses that fed them.

A tall, thin man, dressed in top hat and tails of sparkling crimson, pushed the cemetery's front gate open with a mournful creak. An eerie wind whistled through the twisted, tangled trees as he picked his way through the mazy paths. A pair of half-moon spectacles sat on his long thin nose, and his hair poked out from behind his ears in little curls. He carried a large bouquet of multi-coloured roses under one arm.

A couple of other mourners, wearing customary black, stared at him as he passed, wondering why he was so extravagantly dressed. But he ignored them all, confident in his manner and stride. He was Doctor Barton Bigelow, of Dr Bigelow's Bizarre Bazaar, and he didn't care what other people thought of him.

He knelt beside one of the more recent graves, the headstone newly laid and not yet covered with the cemetery's ever-present moss. He laid down his roses and bowed his head. The headstone read: "Louisa Bigelow, beloved wife of Jake and mother of Nathaniel and Barton".

However, Louisa hadn't been Dr Bigelow's biological mother. She hadn't been present at his birth. Barton had no idea who his real parents were, and no desire to find out. Louisa would always be his real mother, as she had adopted him and raised him as her own son.

Dr Bigelow closed his eyes and remembered. Of course he couldn't recall events he hadn't been a part of, but Louisa had told him her story, and he could fill in the rest himself.

* * *

Louisa Bigelow was a good woman, a kind and gentle soul, who sadly lived in a world of prejudice and scorn. Even though she'd been born into poverty, her family were still a narrow-minded and intolerant lot. When she dared to have a baby out of wedlock, her family immediately booted her out of their tumbledown shack and told her to find her own way in the world.

Louisa Bigelow, aged eighteen, beautiful with long wavy blonde hair and a slender figure despite the days-old child in her arms, staggered up the steep road to the Mojo County Orphanage. Even now the building stood like a grim sentinel on the edge of the crater. It had once been a grand country house, painted white, with green shutters on the windows and neatly-cultivated gardens. But now the rambling weatherboard dwelling was run-down and faded, missing shutters and surrounded by weeds.

Louisa had only the clothes on her back, and her crinoline whispered around her legs as she stopped at the gates of that forbidding building. A cold wind blew down from the hill, but she pulled the tattered woollen shawl from her shoulders, not caring that her thin arms were bare beneath. She wrapped the baby in her scarf and held him up so she could look at him one last time in the pale light of the winter moon.

He was a plump, well-formed little child, but he had a large distinctive wine-stain birthmark on his face. It resembled the markings of a creature called a cheetah, just like the pictures she'd once seen in a book about a faraway world called deepest darkest Alkebula. Louisa was sure, had her son come out unmarked, her father wouldn't have been *quite* so furious with her. Perhaps he would even have convinced her mother to take him and bring him up as her own baby. Thus they could have stayed with the family.

But her father had called her "demon slut", and the baby "demon spawn", and ordered her to take the child away before he killed them both.

Louisa thought the boy's strange mark only made him more beautiful. He opened big blue eyes, as blue as Louisa's own, and started to whimper.

Louisa cuddled him close. "Hush now. Don't you cry, my little wine-stained boy, my sweet Nathaniel. The folks at the orphanage will take good care of ya. They'll fill yer belly with good food, keep yer warm in winter and dry in the rain." She sniffed, and tears started to trickle down her cheeks. "I'll be back fer ya when I make enough money to git us a good home an' a good life. You wait fer me now, Nathaniel."

Louisa hurried up the overgrown path to the orphanage's veranda and ascended the creaky, termite-infested stairs. She put down the basket she'd brought with her and carefully placed the swaddled baby inside. She made sure he was warm and comfortable in her shawl.

"Now you be a good boy, an' don't git inta no trouble," she whispered to him, and placed a kiss on his smooth forehead. She pinned a note to the scarf that read: "My name is Nathaniel. Please look after me."

Louisa scuttled from the veranda, feeling like the worst criminal in the world as she abandoned her newborn son on that dusty old doorstep and hurried off into the night. She hung her head as she headed back out onto Boneyard Way, letting tears flow down her cheeks and sobs tear through her slender body. She had carried little Nathaniel in her belly for nine months, and leaving him behind made her feel like she'd just given birth a second time. Only now, there was no joy of a tiny wriggling life in her belly, nor the thin wails of a new creation to love and hold.

*　*　*

Down in the centre of Mojo Town was the Mule Train Depot. Back in the old days the train was hauled by actual mules, but when all the horses and donkeys died out, their infertile offspring disappeared too. All forms of transportation were forced to become mechanised. The Mule Train was now a trackless device, but change had never come easily to Mojo County's conservative occupants, so the name Mule Train Depot remained. The old sign, faded and pocked with bullet holes, still endured, hanging above the building.

As it was now well after 11 o'clock at night, the Mule Train Depot was locked and quiet. The moon that had lit Louisa's way had disappeared behind dark clouds, and an icy drizzle settled in. Louisa wrapped her arms around her bare shoulders and huddled under the eaves, awaiting the trackless train that would take her to Bhigge Smoche. She had heard that anyone, even a homeless eighteen-year-old from the sticks, could make their fortune there.

Louisa had managed to save a few bucks from doing odd jobs around town by hiding them beneath a loose floorboard under her bed, and she hoped they'd be enough for a ticket and maybe a night or two in a cheap city flophouse. All she needed was a couple of days to find a job, and then she could start her life.

The first train didn't arrive until five in the morning, and Louisa sank down against the wall, using the many layers of her dress to keep warm. Thus she was able to fall into a dreamless doze until the rattle and rumble of the approaching machine stirred her awake. The depot had opened, and she rushed to buy her ticket. The surly attendant didn't bat an eyelid at her dishevelled state—waifs like her were always trying to escape Mojo Town.

The trackless train appeared, a hellish steel beast surrounded by a thick cloud of smoke and steam issuing from the squat chimney at its back. Despite its name, it wasn't really a trackless device. It had six articulated arms, three on each side, ending in vicious claws. The arms at the front lay down tracks for the massive steel device to roll over. At the back two more arms picked up the smoke-blackened tracks and passed them over the top of the machine to the middle set of arms, which ferried them back to the front. The machine continually cycled like this, laying and collecting its own tracks. Thus there was no need to build long and expensive train lines that needed to be maintained and repaired whenever there was an indian attack. The arms were also designed to shift obstacles from the machine's path: boulders, fallen trees, dead animals. It could move backwards as well as forwards, and turn around in a relatively small area. It was similar in design to a mining gripper, but much bigger and faster.

The trackless train slammed its last track down and rolled to a stop at the depot. "All out for the end of the line—Mojo Town!" shouted the conductor. Grey-faced, grey-clad people began to clamber down the ladders and shamble off into the early morning: traders and workers, and a few miserable individuals who'd tried to seek their fortune in

Bhigge Smoche—and failed.

"All aboard!" shouted the conductor as soon as the last person had left. "Make sure you have your tickets ready!" Louisa scrambled up the ladder, and a few other people boarded after her. She made herself comfortable in a seat by the window, and the trackless train rolled out of Mojo Town half an hour later. Shadows cast by its articulated arms began to move across her field of vision. She wasn't sorry to see the last of Mojo's drab, tumbledown dwellings, but then she spotted the hill at the back of town, the orphanage perched high on top, the place where she had left her baby boy.

A cold steel band of grief closed around her chest, and fresh tears burned her eyes. "Mummy loves you," she whispered.

CHAPTER 2

Up at the Mojo County Orphanage, the front door creaked open and a jaundiced gaslight glow illuminated the little baby in his basket.

"Zak! Someone's abandoned another young'un on our stoop!" exclaimed a high-pitched female voice.

"So that's what that racket was!" cried a deeper male voice from within the house. "I thought it was just them blasted rats on our porch again."

"Lucky I came out to check. A bub this small couldn't've lasted more'n an hour or two in this cold." A large woman appeared in the doorway, swathed in a voluminous pink wool dressing gown. She was elderly, with iron-grey hair pulled into a severe bun at the back of her head. A few curls had managed to work their way loose to form little snakes around her face. She would have appeared motherly, had her dark eyes not possessed such an intense predatory gleam as she picked up the baby from his crib and turned to show him to the man behind her. "D'you know what we have here, brother dear?"

The man rubbed his bony hands together with glee. "You betcha, Sissy... That there is gonna be the next star of the show!" He gave a leer, his eyes just as dark and ravenous as his sister's. He had slicked-back black hair, a pencil moustache, and a long thin beard with a curl at the end. He was dressed in silk pyjamas.

Serena "Sissy" Spindler leered back. "This little'un is gonna make us a bundle o' dough."

"Oh yeah, we's gonna rake it in, Sis."

"We'll haveta take special care of this little tyke. Put him on the treatment first thing tomorrow morning. What d'ya think it'll do to him? We've never tried it on a newborn before."

"I dunno, Sis, but it sure is gonna be fun findin' out!" Zachariah "Zak" Spindler cackled with laughter and rubbed his hands together again.

Sissy joined in his glee as she carried the baby down the long, gloomy hallway. "I'll just put him safely to bed in the nursery..."

* * *

Sissy stomped into the bathroom, a dark and cavernous chamber with spiders living in the corners and mould stains all over the walls. The sink was full of hairs, and the floor creaked ominously beneath her heavy tread. She stopped in front of the cracked old bathroom mirror, took a deep breath, and removed her big, thick dressing gown. Beneath it she was wearing a huge pair of bloomers, patched, with loose threads dangling. She frowned at her old, wrinkled reflection in annoyance, and spent a few minutes wondering where her youth and beauty had gone. Then, from the side of the sink she selected a scalpel. She tugged on a thin growth of skin, attached to her belly like a tiny tentacle, and quickly sliced it off. Blood trickled from the wound. She tossed the skin into a bin on the floor.

Zak, who'd come in behind her to use the crapper, pulled a face. "Ya gotta be more careful handling the Stuff—it's givin' ya all them weird growths."

Sissy found another protuberance near her hip and cut it off as well. She gave no sign that she was in any pain. "Ya fergit, Zak, that I was a registered nurse in the Constitutional Army. I was trained ta treat gunshots, whiplash, and fleabites. I could dig a bullet from a soldier's ass as easily as I could clean out a maggoty wound or sew up a bayonet slash. I treated fevers, venereal diseases, and even a fella who'd been run over by one o' those mechanical hosses. So I can *certainly* treat somethin' as trivial as a few knotty skin tags!" She whipped off a third little pseudopod from her thigh.

Zak decided it was best not to argue. He pulled up his silk pyjama pants and flushed the ancient toilet with a gurgle. "Ya know, Sissy, this has gotta be our best scam yet. Untraceable. An' with you being a nurse an' all, we finally got respectability. It's perfect."

Sissy turned to look at him and gave a leer. "Remember tha one we had goin' down south?"

Zak grimaced as he joined her at the sink and hunted around for his toothbrush. "Do I! I almost got bit m'self…"

* * *

Years earlier, Zak, more muscular and with thicker hair up top, had been enjoying a good career as a snake handler. He stood on an ornately draped stage wrestling a very large rattler while, down below, True Believers wailed in delirium. Back then he'd been known as the Reverend Zachariah.

"Trust in the infinite spirit and no harm will come to ye!" Zak thundered in an impressive showman's voice.

"I believe!" wailed a fat middle-aged man as he fell to his knees in front of Zak. He ripped open his shirt to reveal his flabby, pale belly.

The audience whooped and shouted.

"Praise tha all knowing!"

"I believe."

"Hal'luya!"

With practised ease, Zak flipped the infuriated snake around, and it lunged at the fat man's exposed flesh, sinking its fangs in. The man gasped in pain.

Lurking in the shadows at the back of the tent was Sissy, dressed in her Constitutional Army nurse's uniform. She was younger and thinner, but already possessing that hard, calculating look in her eyes. It was her job to milk all the snakes beforehand so their fangs had no effect. Thus it looked like the worshippers' faith had rendered them immune to the venom. "Stupid idjits," Sissy muttered under her breath.

* * *

Sissy couldn't find any more growths, so she dabbed some alcohol on the wounds. Strangely enough, they were almost closed, days' worth of healing in minutes. "We were makin' darn good money outta those suckers till ... the incident."

* * *

One of Zak's snakes was a particularly ornery varmint. Instead of biting the True Believer on the chest or belly, where it was supposed to, it went for his nose—and ripped it clean off his face!

"He was a sinner, my people—an evildoer of vile deeds!" Zak told the audience in his loud persuasive showman's voice. Although he managed to placate most of his followers, some of the more sceptical folk stopped believing his lies and organised a posse.

* * *

"I tended to the fella's wounds and he lived, but I just wasn't good enough to stitch his nose back on," said Sissy. "He was left with two gapin' holes in his face. What was worse, he was an actor, so that kinda ruined his career." She snorted. "We really hadda hightail it outta there, didn't we? 'Fore them folks tried ta string our hides up!"

Zak laughed. "No fear of that now, Sissy."

Sissy joined in with his laughter. She reached for her pink dressing gown and slipped it back on. "Ta think tha county actually *pays* us ta run this here orphanage."

Zak's smile faded. "They don't pay near enough."

Sissy turned on him. "Well, of course it ain't enough when ya gamble it all away ev'ry time the Watkins Desertboat floats inta town, yer dang good-fer-nuthin' fool!" She wagged a bony finger capped with a long pointy nail in his face.

Zak lifted his hands. "Now, now, Sissy, don't get all ornery on me. Ain't a man entitled to a little fun?"

Sissy glared at him and embedded her fists in her meaty hips. "Not when you lose everything we worked hard fer, you ain't!"

Zak backed off. "All right, Sissy, I hear ya, I hear ya. Don't get all steamed up. Best we git some sleep. We gotta a lotta work ta do tomorra."

CHAPTER 3

The trackless train thundered east across the rocky, uneven ground. Every so often it stopped to let people on and off at various shanty-towns, or to remove a large dead animal or smooth over a particularly rough patch. It didn't run that fast, managing to maintain a sedate thirty miles per hour, but the constant clickety-clack, clickety-clack of its moving tracks soothed most of its occupants into deep, dreamless sleep.

However, as was often the case with communal transport, it attracted a collection of unsavoury characters, seeking to escape various demons of the past. And as was also common with such semi-human creatures, they believed the world owed them a living and a little fun at someone else's expense. One particularly fetid thing, who hadn't seen water since baptism and who'd been wearing the same ragged, filthy coat for the last ten years, crept like a plague from his seat across the aisle to where Louisa slumbered uneasily against the window, troubled by dreams about her abandoned child.

"Come an' sit ova 'ere by me, luv," the creature crooned in what it assumed was a soft, seductive voice. It was, in reality, a sibilant hiss from hell. A gnarly hand, festooned with warty growths from numerous untreated illnesses, reached across and pulled at her torn skirt, the cloth she'd removed to use as an impromptu scarf.

Louisa tugged the material around her more closely, trying to ignore the unwanted advances from the stinking mutant, but he persisted, breathing his foul firewater breath all over her. In her half-conscious delirium she flailed away the groping fingers, but they kept coming back to paw her skirts and grope around for her bare flesh.

A newly-arrived passenger noticed her distress and came to her aid. "Pardon me, sir, but yer smellin' up the place sumthin' awful and givin' this poor young lady the vapours. Please displace yer disgusting personage toward the back of the carriage b'fore I do sumthin' you'll regret."

This passenger loomed over the rummy mutant, staring him down with cold, steely eyes. He grinned broadly.

Curled almost foetally to present the smallest possible surface area to the cruel world, Louisa didn't realise that this particular passenger was pointing a small silver pistol into the mutant rummy's bloated belly. It had originally been secreted up his sleeve, but was now extended into his hand via an ingenious mechanical device.

The rummy hurriedly flopped back into his seat, pale and gleaming with sweat. Quick and sleek, the pistol zipped back up the passenger's sleeve, disappearing from sight before anyone else could spot it.

The stranger turned to the now wide-awake Louisa with a smile. He stood tall, well-built and handsome, wearing a black frock coat, an expensive shirt, and a silkshot waistcoat. "Sorry 'bout the disturbance, ma'am. Far too much riff-raff around these parts. Hope yer have a pleasant trip." He tipped his broad-brimmed hat to her, then turned to leave.

"Wait." Louisa looked around, noting all the other sleazy characters on the train. More drunken mutants swathed in foul smelling rags; a heavily-rouged woman of the night practically spilling out of her corset; seedy-looking youths who looked about to embark on a life of crime in the big city. There certainly hadn't been so many before, when she'd boarded the train at Mojo Town. She looked pleadingly up at the handsome gent. "Please, won't ya sit down? I could sure use the company."

"Well, that's mighty kindly of yer, ma'am. So long as I ain't a bother to ya, I'd be delighted." He slipped into the seat next to Louisa, and she inhaled his sweet cologne, like ambrosia after the fetid stench from that raggedy mutant.

The gent tipped his cowboy hat again. "Mah name is William Finemore McCade."

"I'm Louisa Bigelow." She extended a hand to him and he took it, planting a warm kiss on the back.

"Pleased to meet you, Miss Bigelow. Might I ask, what's a fine young lady like you doin' on such a devilish contraption as this? You should be travellin' by private stage."

"Unfortunately, I didn't have the funds fer a private coach." Louisa showed him the scarf she'd made from part of her skirt. "I have but tha clothes on my back and only fifty bucks to my name."

"I am sorry to hear that, ma'am, I really am. I'd like to help you out, but I spent my last dime on a ticket for this here train." He spread his hands. "I'm on my way to Bhigge Smoche. There's a big poker tournament about to start, and I want in on the action."

"Don't those things cost a lot to enter?" Louisa asked.

"Of course, ma'am. The only wealth I have left to my name is a pocket watch that was owned by my pappy and his pappy before him. It's what's gonna get me inter the game." He drew it from a pocket of his waistcoat and showed her. It had several faces: the first showed the time, the second predicted the weather, and the third was a compass. It was wound by a winding crown.

"That's very nice," Louisa approved, and he tucked it back into his pocket before any of the lowlifes noticed it. "Why don't ya show me some card tricks? I seen a few in my time. My brother was quite good at cards, although whatever he won he always spent down at the saloon."

"Of course." McCade produced a well-used deck and showed Louisa some of his moves. He was slick at shuffling the cards, flipping them from one hand to the other and back again. He showed her how to cheat at a game of "Find the Lady", and how to find any card hidden within a deck at first go. The hours started to fly by.

"If I may ask, Miss Bigelow, why are you on yer way to Bhigge Smoche?"

"I'm gonna seek my fortune, Mr McCade. There was nothin' left for me in that backwater hick town. I need to make some money so I can git my little boy Nathaniel back." Tears burned her eyes again, but Louisa blinked them back, vowing to be strong from now on. She would need a heart of steel to survive. "I left him at the Mojo County Orphanage."

"Sounds to me like there's a cur out there somewhere who needs to own up to some fatherly responsibility," growled McCade.

"Oh, yes sir, I completely agree. I thought that lowdown snake-in-the-grass loved me, but when he learned I was in tha family way, he skipped town on this very train, about six months ago. I have no idea where he went."

"What's his name?"

"Jonathan Gale. But when I went round town askin' after him, no one knew who I was talkin' about. Lyin' skunk."

"Oh yeah, fella definitely deserves a whippin', no doubt about that, leavin' a fine lass like you."

"So I wanna make enough for a life for myself an' Nathaniel." Suddenly Louisa remembered something, and reached into the top of her corset, where she kept her secret stash of money and a few other items.

She pulled out a sepia lumograph. "I gotta picture of him."

McCade looked down at the little boy with the wine-stain birthmark on his face, shaped like the markings of a cheetah. "Why, he's just adorable."

"Ya think so? Ya don't think he's a devil's child on account o' that mark on his face?"

"We all got marks in some form or another. I have one in a rather indelicate place, shaped exactly like a cactus." He grinned, and Louisa laughed. She put Nathaniel's lumograph away.

"You thought about what you gonna do in Bhigge Smoche?" asked McCade. "Girl needs to have some skills to survive in the big city."

"Well, I kin read an' write, and I know some arithmetic, too. I taught all my brothers. I know how to sew clothes, I kin cook and clean, and I'm in good health despite what I just went through birthin' Nathaniel. I figger I'll find somethin' I can do."

"You got the right attitude, ma'am. I'm sure you'll do just fine."

At that moment the conductor appeared to announce that the next stop was Bhigge Smoche, and the end of the line.

McCade slid a card from his deck into her hand. It was the Ace of Spades. "Have this to remember me by, lovely lady. I'm gonna be famous all over Westerillo." He stood up, tipped his hat to her, and went off to fetch his luggage.

*   *   *

The trackless train stopped at a grand terminus for mechanical carriages and other trains. Louisa alighted and for a few minutes wandered around wonderstruck, unable to believe that such a fantastic place even existed. Impossibly tall buildings towered overhead, with a veritable spider web of clotheslines and electrical cables tangled between them. Overhead rails for local trams added to the confusion. The sky was dark with smog, and in the distance a forest of tall chimneys rose from various manufactories. And the noise! Louisa had never heard the like! The screeching and thundering of the various mechanical transports, the shouting of people, the distant roar from those manufactories—she wondered if she would ever get used to such a racket.

"Outta the way there, darlin'!" someone shouted, and Louisa realised that she was standing in the way of a grand transport that was about to depart. This one was also a trackless train, but instead of possessing mechanical arms that moved its tracks around its body, it had two enormous articulated treads, some with squashed bits of roadkill still embedded in them. Two great chimneys at the back added to the pollution.

Louisa gathered her skirts and quickly scuttled to the side. Great big crinolines weren't particularly useful for moving around in such crowds, and she realised that she would need to invest in narrower, more practical skirts. Perhaps she could even get one of those new-fangled bustle things. But first things first—she needed to find somewhere to stay.

She bought a *Bhigge Smoche Times* from a seedy-looking paperboy and asked him where she might find modest accommodation. With a wicked leer, the kid directed her to Rundowne Street, a few blocks over. Louisa followed his instruction, heading through the tall grim buildings into a particularly unsavoury part of town that lay in the shadow of the manufactories. *Well, I did ask for cheap*, she thought darkly. *Beggars can't afford to be choosers. Heart of steel*, she told herself. *Heart of steel.*

Due to the manufactories' close proximity, the buildings were grim and smoke-blackened, their windows fogged with soot. Shabbily-dressed people shambled along the footpaths and lurked in the door-ways. Their clothes and faces were grey from the smog, and everyone seemed to have a hacking cough. Some simply slouched on the sidewalks, staring glassily ahead, uncaring of their surroundings. They looked like they were dreaming with their eyes open, and Louisa wondered what they had drunk to intoxicate them so.

Rats the size of armadillos fossicked for food in the garbage-filled gutters. But there, up ahead, was exactly what she was looking for. The Rundowne Arms Hotel advertised rooms for a dollar per night. Three prostitutes, even more scantily-clad than the one from the train, lounged outside and eyed her disdainfully as she ascended the stairs into a grim, murky interior, lit only by flickering gaslights. No matter—she knew how to get along without electricity. Only a few houses at the centre of Mojo Town had ever bothered with that newfangled wire-power. She paid a gap-toothed desk clerk for a week's worth of accommodation, and he directed her up a creaky, dangerous-looking staircase.

Roaches the size of canaries scuttled for cover as soon as Louisa opened the warped wooden door to her room. It was barely large enough for the narrow swaybacked bed and cupboard inside. The sheets looked like they hadn't been washed since … ever. Although she hung them out of the window and bashed most of the bed bugs out of them, tiny bites still bothered her throughout the night.

* * *

Early the next morning, seated in the hotel's filthy little dining room eating a bowl of sludgy grey porridge, Louisa looked through the paper for a suitable job. Her hopes started to sink as she realised that most companies wanted actual formal qualifications. Being from a hick town from the backwoods, she had no paperwork of any kind. And all cooks, cleaners and seamstresses needed to know how to use various newfangled mechanical devices: gas ovens, steam mops, and sewing machines. She'd never even *seen* such technology, let alone known how to operate it! She did see plenty of barmaid and saloon girl jobs, but right now she thought she could do better.

But then, near the bottom of the page, she noticed a large advertisement in bold type:

"Famous Inventor Extraordinaire Sidney Chrome requires motivated assistant to sell his wondrous contraptions to the public. Will be well paid for each sale. No prior training or experience necessary!"

It sounded too good to be true.

Louisa went out, bought herself a new dress to replace her torn old crinoline, and then took one of the overhead trams to the inventor's address. He lived in a far cleaner part of town, where the streets were swept clean and only water flowed down the gutters. She spotted his townhouse almost immediately. It was the one with the big electric light above the front door, and the highly polished shingle that read "Sidney Chrome, Inventor Extraordinaire".

Louisa knocked on his door and, as it swung inwards, a great smoke-cloud escaped. The inventor appeared, dressed in a grubby lab coat, black rubber gloves, and a large steel helmet with various dials, lights, and buttons on his head. "Hello? How can I help you?" He squinted at her through thick spectacle attachments that hung down from the cap.

"Er, my name is Louisa Bigelow. I'm here fer the sales job."

Suddenly Sid whipped the steel hat off. "Whoops! Forgot I still had the brainwaver on! It helps me think." Beneath, his thick red hair frizzed out alarmingly. It still had wires from the machine caught in it. He had a bushy moustache to match and wide, manic eyes. One was green. The other was pink and twisted around, so it was peering sideways. It looked artificial. "You're here for the job, you say?" He whipped off one of his gloves, revealing a mechanical hand with clockwork joints, and poked the pink eye back into position with a click.

"Yes."

He stuck out his mechanical hand to her. "You're hired!"

"I am? So fast?" Dubiously, Louisa took the steel fingers. They were well-lubricated with engine grease.

He pulled his glove back on. "Of course! That ad's been in the paper for months and you're my first applicant!"

"Surely not!" Louisa looked for somewhere discreet to wipe her fingers.

"All the locals know me, and no one wants to work for me." He lowered his voice to a conspiratorial whisper. "Everyone thinks I'm crazy! Just 'cause I blew up my last assistant!"

"Er," said Louisa, suddenly having second thoughts. But then Sid grabbed her arm in that powerful mechanical claw and yanked her into his dim, smoky house. The door slammed behind her, and she found herself in a close, cluttered interior: walls filled from floor to ceiling with teetering shelves of boxes crammed with nuts, bolts, screws, gauges, valves, gears, cogs, wires, and every other conceivable machine part under the sun. She had to turn sideways as Sid pulled her through the labyrinthine corridors of the house and into a room at the back where the smoke was thickest. He fanned it out of the way as he entered a no less cramped space, where half-finished devices had been set up on benches and more steel shelves lined the walls. Boxes of equipment had even been attached to the ceiling. Illumination was provided by electric lights, and at the back of the room an open door led out to a small, cluttered yard.

A clockworker, the silk skin on her face torn and stitched back together in places, half her horsehair wig blackened and missing, was hosing out flames on one of the benches with foam from a large bottle. The robot was dressed in the ragged remains of a once-fine red wool gown, and she twitched and chattered as she worked.

Louisa had to tear her gaze from the thing. She had heard of clockworkers, but had never actually seen one. "How … how do ya *eva* find anything in here, Mr Chrome?" she gasped.

"I know where everything is," answered Sid cheerfully as he pulled her into the middle of the room and up to the back, where he opened a large cupboard. He tapped his forehead. "That's what the brainwaver's for. It gives me total recall. Without it I tend to lose track a little, and then I need to ask Betty for help." He gestured to the clockworker, who'd managed to pat the last of the flames out with her dress. "But I digress. This is what I need you for. To sell my very latest invention. I'm

a little short of funds, you see, and I'm hoping this wonderful contraption will set me up on Easy Street."

There actually was an Easy Street in Bhigge Smoche. It was located up north in the financial district and all the bigwigs, including Big Daddy Watkins, had their massive mansions there.

Sid gestured towards the things cramming the cupboard. They looked like steel tanks on frames that could be worn on the back. They had long hoses attached to tubes that ended in wide nozzles. There was a control board at the back of the tank, with various switches and dials to measure pressure and capacity, and a couple of buttons where the hose became the tube.

Louisa had no idea what she was looking at. "Wh...what... Please excuse my ignorance, Mr Chrome, but I have *no idea* what in tarnation that is."

Sid grinned maniacally. "That, my dear, is my latest invention! Mops are all well and good for washing boards and tiles, but how do you get carpets clean? Little ones can be hung outside and bashed, but that's slow and time-consuming. This device will revolutionise carpet cleaning!" He pulled one out and yanked a cable from the back, plugging it into a wall socket. He shouldered on the pack, activated the contraption with a roar, and started pushing the nozzle across the ragged, threadbare carpet beneath his shoes.

It was fortunate his lab's carpet was so filthy—Louisa could actually see the machine working, making clean stripes across the floor. Dust, dirt, old screws, hair, and other detritus rattled as it was pulled into the big steel tank and spun around at a frightful speed. "That's amazing!" she cried over the racket.

Then he accidentally ran the nozzle over the hem of her skirt and sucked the cloth in. She squealed and tried to yank it free. But the machine had a good grip, and she could feel the material starting to tear.

"Whoops!" Sid flicked a button on the suction tube, and the machine died with an asthmatic wheeze. "Sorry about that, ma'am. But you get the idea. It really is simple to use, and for those households not yet wired for power, it has a back-up clockwork engine that can be wound to last for an hour. It doesn't suck as well, but it still works better than one of those old-fashioned rug-beaters! And when the tank's full, it can be removed and emptied." He took the machine from his shoulders, showing her how to detach the tank and open it. He went outside and poured the contents over the fence into his neighbour's yard.

"It is quite amazing, Mr Chrome!" Louisa declared. "What do you call it?"

He lifted a gloved finger to answer, and then paused. "Actually, I haven't decided. It could be the Vacuum Machine, or the Dust Devil Destroyer, or the Dust Sucker or the Dust Eater or the Dust Collector or the 'Eat My Dust' Machine!"

Louisa snorted. She was starting to like this quite obviously completely insane inventor. "I do like the 'Eat My Dust' Machine."

He grinned. "Pick the name you think will work best and help you sell it. I have five here for you to start with. Try to get at least a hundred for each vacuum, but I'll accept seventy-five."

CHAPTER 4

Louisa Bigelow accepted the job on a commission basis. Sid Chrome would pay her $15 from every sale between $75 and $100, and $20 from every sale at $100 and over. As the average Bhigge Smoche barmaid only made $5 per day at the most, this was a very generous wage.

Unfortunately, convincing people to buy Sid's contraption was another matter. Louisa dolled herself up as prettily as she could and tried to peddle his mechanical device from door to door. But even though Bhigge Smoche city folks were used to seeing complicated machines every day, surrounded as they were by elevated trams, mechanical horses, trains, and clockworkers, they were still sceptical of new fandangled devices. As Louisa pulled Sid's cart full of 'Eat My Dust' Machines through the streets, she realised there were inventors all over the place. They would hang up their shingles, create dodgy devices, suck in investors, swipe their hard-earned cash and then, when their machines invariably exploded in spectacular fashion, they would vamoose without trace.

Although Louisa tried to explain that Sid's device was the real deal, door after door was slammed in her face before she could even hand out a flyer, let alone demonstrate the device. Even when she was invited into a house, it was usually by a lonely pervert who was more interested in the wares beneath her dress than the ones in her cart.

Despite her best efforts, her excellent sales pitch, and her attractive appearance, Louisa failed to sell a single vacuum cleaner. Trudging through the streets every day left her exhausted, and the bad city air soon laid her low with a hacking cough that refused to leave. Reluctantly, she told Sid that she just didn't have the strength to do the work anymore.

He was disappointed to lose her, and gave her $20 for her two weeks' worth of work.

* * *

Louisa tried for other jobs. She did manage to get some work in a perfume shop, but the other girls soon became jealous of her beauty and easy-going manner, and contrived to get rid of her after only a few days. She managed to lie her way into a cleaning job, but couldn't control the electric floor-mopper, and it raced off and crashed through a wall. The owner made her pay for the damage before dismissing her. Eventually, down to her last few Lincoln-skins, she swallowed her pride and took work as a barmaid in a dive on Skidde Rouh, a filthy little lane around the corner from Rundowne Street.

It was called the Buckhorn Palace Saloon. Although it had once been a grand tavern built for the manufactory workers, it was now almost exclusively inhabited by full-time winos and rummies. The bar had been wired, but its lights flickered intermittently, illuminating a grim and filthy chamber crammed with deros who slobbered and exhaled their foul breath all over Louisa as she scurried to and fro across the rotten, creaking floorboards. She tried not to think about how low she had sunk, forcing herself to concentrate on the pennies she made, the money she wanted to put aside for her new life with Nathaniel.

At least she wasn't one of the pale skinny whores who loitered around the edges of the barroom, watching the drunks through desperate black-ringed eyes. Occasionally a less-intoxicated patron would close an arm around one of these women and drag her off to one of the various small rooms up the creaking stairs. At least Louisa received a regular wage of $5, plus whatever tips the sots managed to dig from their unwashed pockets.

For a while, Louisa Bigelow survived as the Buckhorn Palace Saloon's best barmaid. She managed to save a few dollars, get her grimy little hotel room cleaned, and even purchase a few new frocks. She began to feel that she was getting somewhere, moving towards her new life with Nathaniel.

But to make the kind of money she needed would take a long, long time at such a low-paying job. And frankly, she hated it: the dirty, lustful drunks; their inane slurred conversation; the lack of any change in her dull routine. After a few weeks her confident mood started to slip.

Every day, on her walk to work, she'd pass a two-headed Duoquois indian who lurked in the shadows between the Buckhorn Palace and the Sweet Sugar Shack, a small but popular sweet store and bakery. At first, the sight of the two-headed copper-skinned native—covered with tattoos, and dressed in nothing but a beaded loincloth, carrying a buckskin bag slung over one shoulder—frightened her. But since then, she'd grown used to the sight of Duoquois indians—they were the only natives who ever dared to enter the city. They didn't mind the world of the pale faces, or making their living exploiting their numerous weaknesses.

No one knew the Duoquois' real name—all the locals simply called him the Indian Giver. Inside his buckskin bag he carried a pouch of Mescala worms. Louisa had seen people surreptitiously scurry up to him and hand over $5 notes for them, and then hurry off just as quickly, sucking on these small green creatures. When Louisa had asked Jake, one of the saloon's less disgusting regulars, what was going on, he informed her that the worms' skins were poisonous, but in small doses produced a hallucinogenic euphoria much stronger than the buzz from alcohol.

For a while, the weak and weary could forget their worries by entering a dreamlike state that made them appear like they were sleeping with their eyes open. Louisa realised that this explained all the down-and-outs she saw slumped in the doorways and alleys, stoned and oblivious to their surroundings and life in general. They slipped into a state known as the Perpetual Dream. When it wore off and the pain of the grim real world started to intrude, all they had to do was suck on the worm again. The tiny creatures lasted twenty-four hours before dying, and then, invariably, the Dreamers, as the addicts were called, would swallow them for one last hit. Often this was the only nourishment they got, and after only a few weeks on the worm they would disappear, presumed by one and all to be dead.

It was a highly addictive drug, but it was possible for an addict to kick the habit and come out of the Perpetual Dream. They wouldn't suffer any debilitating withdrawal symptoms, only the occasional flashback.

Warned by Jake to stay away from the Indian Giver and his tainted merchandise, Louisa would always rush past him with her head down, not wanting to make eye contact with either of his two heads.

Louisa knew Jake was sweet on her. He was a local worker from one of the manufactories. He came to the Buckhorn Palace every afternoon after work, where he downed a few beers before returning to his apartment on nearby Rottenrat Rouh. Unlike his fellow workers, who'd all moved into newer manufactory-owned dwellings, he preferred the area he'd grown up in, even if it had gone to the dogs. He was a tall, well-built fellow with bushy brown hair and rough, work-hardened hands from labouring on the production lines all day. His factory was owned by the Watkins Corporation and built steam engines for mechanical horses and carriages. He was rough and blunt-spoken, but he enjoyed bantering with Louisa, whom he saw as a single light of joy in an increasingly grim and uncaring world.

But Louisa didn't want to become involved with him. Even now, working as a barmaid in such a dirty, low-class establishment, she felt she could do better. She didn't want a lowly manufactory worker who only made a few dollars more than her. She wanted someone better, someone who could sweep her off her feet so she'd never have to work again. She wondered about the handsome man from the trackless train—William McCade—and if he had made his fortune. Sometimes, while carrying slopping beer mugs across the barroom, she'd fantasise about him throwing the saloon's swing-doors wide and marching in to lift her into his arms.

"I've made my fortune and I'm here to take you away from all this squalor, my love," he would proclaim. "I'm sorry it took me so long to find you, but I had no idea where you'd gone."

Occasionally Louisa would take her big jar of tips to a seedy little bank not far from the train terminus and exchange them for notes that were far easier to store. She wanted to open an account, but was informed by the weaselly little manager that she needed a minimum of $100 to do so. So far, she'd only managed to save $25. Of course he did, with a suggestive leer, give her the option to open an account for a considerably lesser amount, but only if she opened her *legs* first.

One night, returning from the bank with her notes stuffed into her corset, Louisa realised she was being followed by some Dreamers who'd used up their worms. Their hungry gazes were fixed and intense. She didn't recognise them—locals tended to leave her alone. These were newcomers, still relatively fit and healthy from whatever they'd been doing before they'd decided to give up on life. Already scruffy and dirty, they stepped into her way as she turned the corner into Rundowne Street.

Louisa knew a few tricks to defend herself, but not against four Dreamers hell-bent on getting enough money for their next fix. She had time for one loud scream for help before they grabbed her and hauled her into a dark alley. She fought like a wildcat, kicking and punching to try and keep them off her, but they were determined to get the money they'd seen her tuck away. Their hands ripped and tore at her clothes, and then the wad of notes was yanked free with a triumphant shriek.

"No, that's *mine*!" Louisa shouted. "*Mine and Nathaniel's*!" She jumped to her feet, but the Dreamers were already scattering down Rundowne Street, disappearing into various doorways and shadows. Louisa howled in despair, cursing and calling the bums every foul name she could think of.

She noticed, not so far away, one of Rundowne Street's many whores watching her with a wicked smirk on her pox-scarred face. Obviously she'd heard Louisa's cry for help and decided not to do a thing about it. "Now yer no better'n us, you snooty slut!" she declared.

This was the last straw! What was her bloody misplaced pride worth now? She'd lost $10 to those Dreamers! She'd never make enough money to get Nathaniel back. Hell, she didn't *deserve* to get him back.

Under her bed, Louisa kept a bottle of rotgut whiskey she'd bought from the Buckhorn Palace. Recently she'd taken to drinking a nip or two before bedtime, just to steady her nerves enough so she could fall asleep. She wasn't anything like a raging alcoholic yet. The bottle was still three-quarters full. But that night she took a good long pull on it, and drained it down to a third.

She woke with a headache, but still managed to drag herself to work the next day. Her boss and, later, Jake could tell something was up, but she fobbed their concerns off. She'd been brought up to keep her problems to herself, and now was no exception.

As soon as she received her pay for the day, she took the $5 to the Indian Giver.

His two heads grinned wickedly at her. "Knew you would come one day," one of the heads declared.

She held out the note. "Just gimme tha damn worm," she growled. The Indian Giver reached into his bag and pulled out one small, wriggly green critter. She snatched it off him without a word of thanks and hurried off.

*　*　*

Back in her little bedsit, Louisa flopped down on her bed and opened her hand, looking at the creature squirming on her palm. It was slimy and disgusting, and she really didn't want to put it in her mouth. But she knew, from the delirious rapture she'd seen on the faces of the Dreamers, that it would help to chase away the pain of her humiliation and failure.

But she needed a little courage first. She didn't want to try sucking on that revolting thing and then throw up in disgust, so she reached under her bed for the bottle of whiskey. She took a long swig from the bottle, draining it dry. She remembered Jake telling her that alcohol and Mescala worms didn't mix, but right now she didn't care. As the room performed a lazy rotation around her head, Louisa lifted the worm by one end and touched it to her lips. She gave its head—at least she hoped it was its head—a very delicate lick.

Nothing happened, so she licked it again. It didn't taste particularly bad. Just meaty. Still nothing.

She put the worm into her mouth and slid it under her tongue. Something had to happen now. She waited.

The room stopped spinning. Then, without warning, the walls fell away like the petals of a flower. Louisa couldn't believe her senses. Outside lay a world with a bright blue sky dotted with fluffy white clouds. A brilliant yellow sun shone down on thick green trees covered with flowers and brightly-coloured fruits. Their branches spread in all directions. Louisa's old swaybacked bed had turned into a grand four-poster bed, and her nightstand had become an elegant dresser. They were perched on a hilltop covered with lush green grass. She'd never seen colours so rich and vibrant. Did worlds like this even exist anywhere in creation?

Oh, if this was what it was like to dream while she was awake, then she could keep on doing it, forever and ever. It was so much better than the drab grey world in which she lived. Louisa turned in the bed to see more of this wonderful new fantasy land. More hills covered with trees, little villages of whitewashed houses nestling in the valleys, birds chirping merrily as they fluttered across the sky.

But then she spotted something in front of her, a part of reality that had managed to intrude. A crumpled lumograph lying on the dresser.

It depicted the small round face of a newborn baby with a strange birthmark on his face, like someone had spilled red wine down his forehead and it had run down both sides of his face.

He looked familiar, but caught up in the wonder of her amazing dream, she couldn't remember who he was…

CHAPTER 5

A year passed. The rundown Mojo County Orphanage continued to loom on the hill overlooking Mojo Town, watching over it like a stern parent watches over its wayward children. The locals continued to ignore it, only acknowledging its existence during the night, when they could leave their unwanted babes on its rotting doorstep in darkness and secret. They saw the brother and sister who ran the place quite regularly in town, and occasionally glimpsed a skinny boy with curly brown hair; but apart from him, they never saw any of the other children.

Were the wee 'uns even still alive in that grim, forbidding edifice? They wanted to know, yet at the same time they didn't. They wanted to keep their heads buried in the sand and pretend that everything was perfectly normal. Otherwise the mayor might close the place down, and then where would they leave their bastard whelps?

The boy with the curly brown hair was called Barton, and he was about ten years old. He couldn't remember his last name, or even if he'd ever had one. He'd spent his entire life at the orphanage and couldn't recall a time beforehand. He was usually dressed in a ragged man's shirt with the sleeves rolled up and a pair of shorts held up with rope.

He was playing fetch with a mangy mongrel dog. It had wandered in from the junkyard a few days ago, but instead of returning it, Sissy had tied it up and given it some food. Bart thought maybe she wanted it to kill rats, so he named it Fido and befriended it.

Fido trotted up to him, obediently dropping a stick at his bare feet, and he picked it up. He threw it again, and with an excited yelp, the dog raced across the yard, his paws scattering the dust into clouds that refused to settle.

* * *

Zak pounded the nail into the wooden sign positioned next to the front door of the orphanage. He tried to straighten it, but it defied his attempts. Sissy's crude lettering was crooked, and no amount of levelling made it look right.

Zak took a step back and scrutinised the sign. It read "Rosewell". What did that mean? He scratched his head in confusion. Another of Sissy's bright ideas, no doubt. Throwing his arms up in resignation, he placed his hammer in the toolbox, picked it up, and went inside.

"Sign's up, Sissy."

"Good," Sissy beamed. "Does it look purdy? Does it make tha place look more homely?"

"Uh-h," Zak stuttered. "It's just a cruddy ol' sign."

Sissy's face immediately turned into a scowl.

"What's it mean, anyway? Rosewell?"

"Neva you mind!" Sissy snapped. "Now put that toolbox away and help with tha meals."

"Yes, Sissy." Zak knew better than to argue. He slunk off.

Sissy went outside to look at her sign. She'd spent hours painting the piece of paling, carefully decorating it with sprigs of flowers and leaves. She stood back and studied it, proud of her handiwork, although in truth the lettering was shaky and the floral design was rather sad and shabby.

As she looked at the sign, she fantasised about when she was young and beautiful. Imagined herself standing on the veranda of a large stately house. Imagined her husband, a young army officer returning home, taking her in his strong arms and kissing her passionately. Imagined a happy home filled with happy laughing children…

The sound of a child laughing and a dog barking broke Sissy's reverie.

"Bart! Stop muckin' around with that stupid dang mutt and tie it back up!" Sissy shrieked from the front porch. "It ain't a pet, and I need ya inside to help with the chores!"

"Sorry, boy," Bart told the dog. "I musta lost track of time a bit." He took Fido by his collar and led him over to the clothesline, where his food and water bowl lay. He tied him back up and patted his head. "I'll try ta come back and play with ya later!" he told him in a conspiratorial whisper. The dog gave a whine and lay down in a patch of shade.

Bart raced back into the house, his small bare feet pattering against the floorboards. Sissy led him into the kitchen at the back, which was full of smoke and steam and the smell of porridge. Sissy dipped a big wooden spoon into a giant pot and stirred it around. "It's just about done," she declared. "Start dishin' it out, Zak, and go easy on the portions. We don't wanna overfeed the ungrateful li'l bastards."

Zak began spooning the gruel into small bowls. "No fear, Sis. I always give 'em the bare min'mum sus'nance they's requirin'." He arranged the bowls on a wooden cart. "On ya way, Bart."

Bart trundled the cart from the kitchen through to the adjoining dining room. The room was crammed with a good percentage of Mojo Town's unwanted children, all lined up and waiting expectantly for their food. They were alive, and dressed and healthy … of sorts. But they weren't the children that had been left behind.

Some of these young'uns may have had club feet and harelips and possibly an extra finger or toe when they were dumped on the doorstep, but that was as far as their deformities had gone then. These children were monstrous creatures, true freaks. One boy had four arms and four legs, and was starting to grow extra eyes. He scuttled along like a spider as he moved forward. Another boy had a huge round body and an enormous mouth. His arms and legs extended from his torso like spindly little sticks. A third boy had abnormally long, thin legs with multiple joints. He moved like a marionette.

There was a girl with multiple heads, and a pair of relatively normal-looking female twins who, instead of hair, had fat tentacles growing from their heads like medusa snakes. Each pseudopod ended in a small human head. A fourth girl had a long, thin body like a snake's, with tiny, spindly little arms. She even moved like a snake as she slithered up to the cart. She licked her lips with a forked tongue in anticipation.

Zak placed a bowl of gruel in front of a boy who could only scuttle about on all fours. He had a huge, wide mouth like a frog's, but filled with lots of sharp teeth. One of his eyes extended from his head on a stalk. "Here ya go, Rex," Zak told him, and patted him on the head. "Don't gulp it all down at once … Enjoy!" Zak chuckled like he'd made the funniest joke in the world, and then straightened up. "Gather round, kids, it's brekky time! Don't eat too fast, or yer might git a bellyache!" He laughed again.

The children, Bart included, cleaned out their bowls with their fingers and various other protuberances, licking them clean. Frankly, Sissy's porridge tasted like Brussels sprouts, boiled dishrags, and old socks, but the orphaned kids couldn't be choosers.

Afterwards, Zak collected all the empty bowls, piling them back on the trolley, and Bart pushed it back into the kitchen and up to the sink. One of the freaks, a girl with four arms who could do the job the

quickest, washed all the bowls and stacked them up.

"Everyone fed?" Sissy asked Zak. "I gotta start the stew for tonight."

"Yup. I's just got Ma an' Pa left ta feed," Zak replied. He turned to Bart. "Come with me, boy—you old enough to help with 'em now."

Bart gulped. He didn't want to see Zak and Sissy's mysterious parents. He knew they occupied the entire top floor of the rambling old house, but they never came downstairs. They were shut-ins.

Zak lurched out into the backyard, Bart following. They headed up the back to a large tumbledown barn. It was full of chickens and pigs—some relatively normal, others grossly mutated. Occasionally, as a treat, Sissy would feed the children meat, but only from the deformed critters. The healthy ones were reserved for the grown-ups.

Zak snatched up a chook and deftly wrung its neck. "Bart, you go'n git Fido."

"B-but whaddaya want with Fido?" Bart stuttered.

Zak loomed menacingly over Bart. "Just do as yer told, brat!"

Bart gulped again and went out to untie Fido. From the sinking feeling in his guts, he realised that this wasn't going to end well.

Zak limped up the steep, creaking stairs that twisted up through the middle of the house. The dead chicken swung in his hand, blood pattering from its beak onto the frayed carpet. Bart followed, pulling on Fido's rope. The dog had obviously never been in a house before, and he barked in protest. His claws scratched against the boards and hooked into the carpet.

"Quit that dang yapping, ya stupid mutt!" Zak thundered at the dog.

Fido ignored him, pulling this way and that. Bart was only small and really had to struggle to control him. They reached the top floor landing, and it was lined with doors, all closed. There was an odd smell in the air, like berries. In fact, it smelled a lot like the wine Sissy and Zak drank in the evenings.

"Come on," Zak growled, and stomped along the landing towards the end.

Fido, by now completely hysterical, skidded along the hallway, dragging Bart behind him.

"Fer Pete's sake, Bart! Control that blasted animal! You don't wanna be upsetting Ma 'n' Pa!"

"I'm tryin', Unca Zak, but he's too big for me!"

Zak opened the door at the end. It led into a conservatory with a high glass ceiling. It was full of vines, and for a moment Bart had no idea what he was looking at. Then he noticed the two mutated giants growing in the middle, soaring almost to the roof. They looked like trees, but had roughly human forms. They had no legs, their torsos growing directly from dirt on the floor, and their arms had changed into leafy branches that had attached themselves to the walls like ivy. Their heads extended on long sinewy trunks that moved like snakes, and their faces were those of an elderly couple: a man and a woman with leaves for hair. Both were drooling in anticipation of the feast. Their bodies were hung with elderberry vines, and large clusters of plump grapes bulged from various places on their bodies.

Bart could only gape in horror at the gruesome sight. He was used to his freakish brothers and sisters, but these two were beyond horrific. He couldn't believe his senses.

"Grub's up, Ma an' Pa!" Zak called. He held out the chicken, and motioned for Bart to bring the dog forward.

Ma and Pa babbled insanely.

"Wicked boy! Wicked, wicked boy!" Ma snarled.

"Where's my cake? I want cake," Pa demanded.

Fido managed to pull himself free from Bart's slack grip and bolt for the door. Ma's head shot forward as fast as a snake's, and a long tongue-vine shot out and wrapped itself around Fido's middle.

"*No!*" cried Bart in horror. He tried to grab the dog's leash to pull him back, but Ma was already yanking him high into the air. Her mouth split open like a flower lined with needle-sharp teeth, and closed around the helpless, yelping creature. She tilted her head back, and the barking became muffled as the dog slid headfirst down her enormous gullet. Her bark-like skin pulsed as she swallowed him whole. His back legs kicked wildly.

Pa snatched the dead chicken from Zak's hand and consumed it in the same manner. But then he coughed and spluttered, vomited up a sticky green goo mixed with feathers.

"Dang it, boy! Don'cha know I'm allergic ta roadrunner?"

Zak rolled his eyes in exasperation. "It's chicken, Pa. Ya et the same dang thing last week, an' said it was the tastiest meal ya eva had! Don'cha remember?"

Pa glared at Zak through a pair of small, piggy green eyes. "Shut yo mouth, boy—don't you be disrespectin' yer elders!"

Fido continued to struggle in Ma's mouth, and he almost slipped back out. She whipped her head back again, and finally he slid down into her stomach and disappeared. She gave a loud gulp and released a thunderous belch.

"Quit flapping yer gums, ya senile old goat!" she shouted at Pa. "Yer upset me lunch! If I get indergestion it'll be your fault!" She burped again, and this time the frayed rope that had been around Fido's neck came up and plopped on the conservatory's dirt floor, all covered with slime.

Zak sniggered. "Yer'll be all right, Ma an' Pa. I'll see ya soon with more fertiliser. This stuff on the floor's gettin' a little thin." He heard the patter of bare feet, and realised that Bart had fled the room. "Dang it! Miserable little brat! Thought he was made o' sterner stuff!"

* * *

Bart raced downstairs and into the library: a large, decrepit old room located at the rear of the house, on the opposite side of the hall from the kitchen and dining room. It was full of dusty old tomes that had been left by the previous owner. Only Bart used it with any regularity,

and weeds had started to push their way in through broken boards and windows. Birds had even started nesting in the rafters and high atop the tall bookcases.

Most of the other children couldn't read or write, and Zak only read newspapers. Sissy wanted to pursue her education, but only in her particular field. She'd already been through the ancient books and read those that interested her. It was Bart who'd been systematically reading and devouring every volume in the place. Despite his tender years, he'd already worked his way through half of the library. He didn't care what he read, although he was starting to develop a particular interest in science.

But today he wasn't interested in selecting a volume to peruse. He tucked himself up in a dark corner at the very back of the room, where cobwebs hung from the ceiling like curtains, and leaves that had blown in from outside littered the floor. He curled himself up in a ball and dissolved into tears. He'd only known Fido for a few days, but during that time he had fallen in love with the dog, and enjoyed every moment he spent with him. To see Fido sacrificed as food to such a revolting creature as Ma rocked him to the core, and his stomach still churned. He wanted to throw up, but knew that if he did, he'd be weak and sick with hunger until dinner.

So he kept his guts under control and stayed in his dark corner, crying and rocking gently back and forth. He didn't realise that someone had come up to him until a soft voice called out, "Bart?"

Bart jumped and blinked away his tears. A boy who looked about six years old was standing over him. He had scruffy blond hair that stood straight up in places, and a weird birthmark on his face. Apart from that, he looked like a perfectly normal boy in his threadbare singlet and faded shorts. But despite his height, he was only about a year old.

"Knewed you'd be 'ere!" he said. "Whatcha doin'?"

"Nuthin'," Bart mumbled.

"Aunt Sissy's bin callin' for ya."

Bart rolled his eyes. "She's always callin' for me."

"She'll get mad if ya don't come."

"Don't care," Bart growled. "Nate, let's you'n me run away from this horrible place. I ... I seen somethin' today that's gonna give me nightmares forever, I reckon."

Nate gaped at Bart in horror. "But we can't leave Aunt Sissy and Uncle Zak!"

Bart got up from his dusty corner and brushed down his shorts. "Why not? They ain't our kin."

Nate continued to stare. "They ain't? How do ya know?"

Bart pressed a hand against his chest. "I just do."

Nate gulped. "But—but where would we go? This is the only place for kids like us. Kids who ... ain't wanted." He touched the strange wine-stain birthmark on his face.

"Anywhere's gotta be better'n here," Bart declared.

"I dunno, Bart." Nate might have grown and learned at a vastly accelerated rate, but he didn't have the emotional maturity of an older child. He cried at the drop of a hat, was frightened of everything, and still had the occasional temper tantrum. Bart had been given the role of caring for Nate, being the big brother he'd never had, and shielding him from the other kids, who could sometimes be incredibly cruel to each other as they established their various pecking orders. Bart had grown to love Nate, and realised he couldn't run away and leave him on his own. The others would eat him alive. He'd have to stay and support him, his only friend in this gawdforsaken place.

The others didn't really like him and Nate. The two boys were far too ... *normal* for them. Bart could have passed for an ordinary Mojo Town lad, and Nate just had that weird birthmark, nothing else.

Where *could* they go, anyway? Mojo Town had nothing to offer a pair of orphaned boys, and the sheriff would quickly make sure they were rounded up and escorted back up here.

This was the only home either of them had ever known.

CHAPTER 6

As Zak limped back into the house after enjoying a smoke out on the back porch, he encountered his sister leading the twin girls with tentacles growing from their heads down the hall towards the stairs. They were both around twelve years old, just about to begin their journey into puberty. Their names were Holly and Ivy. "So how are Ma 'n' Pa today?" Sissy asked conversationally. "Still grizzling?"

"Yup. Surely we coulda found some other guinea pigs ta test the Stuff on…?"

"Yar, I knew it were a mistake ta slip the Stuff into their elderberry juice. But they actually seem happy vegetatin' up there in the conservatory, and they sure do provide us with some mighty fine wine each season!" She gave a wicked cackle.

Zak had to laugh. "You got that right, Sissy. Speakin' of which, I think they's just about ripe for the harvestin'."

"Oh, orright. Might hafta git someone onta that. Right now I gotta give these tykes their treatment. They's *also* ripe for the pluckin'!" Sissy cackled again. "But I need some help. *Bart!*" she shrieked. "Where'n tarnation is that ignorant runt?" She paused at a doorway beneath the stairs. "*Bart! Git'cher scrawny little behind down 'ere pronto!*"

The boys exited the library just in time to hear Sissy hollering. Bart hurried up to her while Nate retreated up the stairs to the first floor, where the kids spent most of their time.

"I bin callin' yer for ages, ya disobedient little brat!" Sissy slapped Bart across the face. "Don'tcha make me wait again!"

"N-no, Aunt Sissy." Tears stung his eyes, but he gulped and forced them back, vowing not to cry. Tears didn't move her; they never had. Best to just placate her and make sure she had no reason to yell at him again. "I'm sorry, Aunt Sissy. I won't do it again."

"Good, 'coz ya the only kid I can rely on to help me without making a dog's breakfast of things." She unlocked a wooden door under the stairs and pulled it open. Stepping inside, she flicked a light switch, revealing a set of steep stone stairs leading down. The rest of the house may have used gas, but she had made sure that this, her secret sanctuary, was wired.

She needed electricity for her work.

At the bottom of the stairs, a long stone corridor ran the length of the house. It was hung with electric bulbs. Various rooms led off from it. In the old days they'd been used as servants' quarters, and to store preserved fruit from the orchard. Now all the rooms on one side had been converted into one large, long laboratory, while the others were used for storage.

One end of the lab was filled with shelves. Some contained boxes of surgical implements and supplies: syringes, scalpels, scissors, needles, cotton, and bandages. Others contained jars bearing preserved specimens of Sissy's more interesting failures. All those unblinking eyes, watching Bart through the murky formaldehyde, gave him the willies.

But he'd been down here before, and knew what to expect. Unlike poor Holly and Ivy, whom Sissy made lie down on two operating tables located under a bright round hospital lamp.

"What'cher gonna do to us, Aunt Sissy?" Ivy asked nervously.

"Don't'choo fret none, Ivy. I'm jus' gonna make you'n Holly better, that's all."

Ivy lifted her hands to the tentacles on her head. "You gonna take these horrid things off? Make me normal-lookin' again?"

"Normal-lookin'? Who wants ta be normal-lookin'? That's dull and borin', that is!" Sissy bustled over to a sink and filled a syringe from a large unlabelled bottle. "And it certainly won't make us any money."

Both Ivy and Holly gaped at Bart in horror. He had a brief vision of grabbing the girls by their hands and making a dash for the stairs, but Sissy was already turning with the big needle in her gnarly hand. She leered as she plunged the needle into Ivy's arm with practised ease. Almost immediately, Ivy's eyes rolled back into her head and she slumped on the steel-topped table. Bart winced and his stomach churned. He hated this part … when the children found out that he was helping Aunt Sissy to mutate them.

Giving them *another* reason to hate him.

But what could he do? If he disobeyed, he'd be beaten, locked up, starved… the list of punishments Aunt Sissy and Uncle Zak had for disobedient kids was endless.

"Ivy!" cried Holly in horror.

"Bart, stop dithering! Strip Ivy, strap her down on her belly, make her comfortable and git the ether flowin'. Don't want her wakin' up durin' the procedure and mussin' all my good work." Sissy filled another needle. "Ya know this stuff is only temp'ry!"

"Yes, Aunt Sissy." Feeling like a complete heel, Bart did as he was told, stretching Ivy out and removing her thin cotton dress and knickers. He slid her slender arms and legs into the leather straps that had been attached to the table and pulled them tight.

Holly turned and tried to run, but Sissy was too quick and caught her. She plunged the needle into Holly as well, and the girl slumped into her arms.

As Sissy was preparing Holly, Bart pulled over a trolley containing two gas canisters fitted with masks. He unhooked one mask and strapped it over Ivy's slack drooling face. He turned the wheel on top, a needle on a dial flickered, and the gas began to flow.

Sissy gave him a gap-toothed smile, genuinely pleased with his cooperation. "Good boy! Now you give Holly the gas while I start workin' on Ivy."

"Yes, Aunt Sissy."

Sissy selected a scalpel from a collection arranged next to the sink and carefully cut away the skin from Ivy's back. Then she did the same thing to Holly, exposing the muscles beneath.

Bart made sure to keep the ether flowing. He stroked the girls' heads as they slumbered uneasily beneath the gas's influence, making sure they didn't wake. He didn't know what he'd do if they stirred and realised the horror that was happening to them.

When Sissy finished baring their muscles and pinning the skin back, she waddled over to the sink and collected a large jar containing about two inches of a glistening green substance. She held it up to the light and frowned. "Not much left. Looks like I'm gonna hafta git sum more." She selected a large spatula from the collection of instruments she'd laid out and dipped it into the jar. It was a thick slime that wobbled like jelly as she lifted a good dose out. Leaning over Ivy, she started to smear the Stuff onto the girl's muscles. There was a soft sizzling sound, and it started to sink into the exposed red flesh.

She did the same thing to Holly.

Meanwhile, tiny green tendrils started to sprout from Ivy's back, looking almost like miniscule bean shoots. Bart was horrified, but couldn't tear his gaze away. The process had always appealed to the clinical part of him, his increasing fascination with science. The part of him that craved comments like, "*Good, 'coz ya the only kid I can rely on to help me without making a dog's breakfast o' things."*

"It's ready! Help me get 'em up!" Sissy barked as she undid Holly's straps and hauled the girl into a sitting position. Holly flopped limply, still unconscious from the flow of ether through the mask on her face.

Bart undid Ivy's straps and lifted her into a sitting position.

Sissy unlocked the wheels on Holly's operating table and rolled it over. "Hold Ivy up!" she ordered.

Bart did so carefully, so the edges of the wounds lined up perfectly, Sissy pressed Holly against Ivy's back. Bart saw the tiny green tendrils at the edges touch and join together.

"Yes, yes, perfect!" Sissy purred. "I was right! The Stuff *is* the most potent just before puberty! Now keep 'em together and unconscious while I stitch 'em up." She went back to her tools and selected a needle and cotton. While Bart held them together and managed to keep the masks secure on their faces, Sissy sewed the wounds shut, turning Holly and Ivy into a pair of Siamese twins joined at the back.

"Now after a week or two, their wounds'll heal and we'll have *another* marvellous freak fer our collection." Sissy rubbed her gnarled hands together with glee. "Aren't they lovely? My latest masterpiece completed!"

Bart took a deep, shaking breath. "Yer a true artist, Aunt Sissy."

"I knows it." She leered, soaking in her own glory. "Now git their masks off and let 'em wake up naturally. I'll take 'em upstairs and show 'em how to move around. I got a mighty fine project lined up for 'em. You clean up the tools and put 'em away. I want everything spick and span for tha next job."

Bart bowed his head, realising that praise for helping her to perform such an abominable experiment was too much to hope for. "Yes, Aunt Sissy."

"An' when yer done in here, take some buckets up to Ma 'n' Pa's room an' pluck their grapes. When yer done that, open a window or two, give 'em sum air, it gets right hot 'n' stuffy in there. We don't want 'em to get all shrivelled and wilty. It'll affect the next brew!"

Bart baulked at the task, but managed to nip his protest in the bud. "Yes, Aunt Sissy."

Sissy took the groggy twins from Bart and placed them gently on their sides on one of the tables. Zak came clattering down the stairs. "I just finished fertilisin' Ma and Pa, but I ain't plucked their grapes yet. Few bunches are up a bit too high for me t'reach with me gammy legs. I need some'un young and agile."

"Bart'll do it once he's finished here. You kin help me git the twins upstairs when they wake up."

While Bart cleaned up, Sissy held up the jar of Stuff to the light again. Now only a thin layer remained.

Sissy frowned. "Not much left after that li'l operation."

"Will there be enough for Nathaniel's treatment?" Zak asked. "It's a pretty big damn job yer wanna do to him. I don't think you've ever tried anythin' that complicated before."

"All I'm doing to Nathaniel fer now is injecting tha Stuff into his pituitary gland ta quicken his growth process. And it's worked wonders, hasn't it? The little scoundrel's only a year old, and already as big an' smart as a six-year-old. He'll hit puberty in no time. I'll finish this bottle off on Nate, then we'll go git sum more." She put the jar up onto a shelf, next to a lot of other jars full of noxious chemicals.

"Righto, Sis."

*　*　*

Bart lugged a step ladder and a bucket up the stairs to the top floor. Gulping, he nudged the door to the conservatory open. The familiar smell of elderberry grapes wafted out, this time mixed with the scent of fresh chicken manure.

Fortunately for the lad, the big meal of dog and chicken, coupled with the fresh new soil, had soothed the mutated oldies into a deep sleep. Both were snoring blissfully, unaware of the boy's presence as he set up his ladder and started harvesting all the juicy-looking ripe grapes. It had been hours since breakfast and his stomach gave a mournful growl. The berries actually smelled really good, better than anything Aunt Sissy had given him. He couldn't wait until tonight's thin stew, which would undoubtedly taste a lot like the breakfast gruel.

Unless, of course, Sissy decided the kids deserved a treat and put some meat into it.

As Bart worked, he popped a few of the hybrid grape-berries into his mouth. They tasted so delicious that for a few minutes he forgot the horrors of the day: the death of Fido and the twins' joining. The berries popped in his mouth like delightful sweet flavour bombs.

Pa rumbled loudly, making sucking noises with his gums in between snores. Bart removed several clusters of grapes from beneath his arms and his stomach, and then the bucket was full. He carried it downstairs, all the way into the kitchen, and emptied it into a vat in the corner. Later, the mutant kids with additional feet would stomp them into juice.

He filled the bucket three more times before all the edible grapes on Ma and Pa were gone and only unripe ones remained. Then he pushed the ladder up to a window. He opened it a crack, and some fresh afternoon air wafted in. He sighed as it cooled his hot skin. It really was a furnace up here.

As Bart was about to pick up the ladder and leave, he noticed a newspaper in one corner, partially concealed under the fertiliser. Zak must have left it up here for Ma and Pa to read. He snatched it up, shook the dirt off it, and skimmed the exciting article on the front page. Deciding to keep it, he folded it small and stuffed it into his oversized shirt. Then he grabbed the ladder and left the snoring oldies to whatever dreams continued to stumble across their warped subconscious.

CHAPTER 7

Early one morning, a few days later, Sissy and Zak carefully picked their way down a steep rocky path into the meteor crater located behind the Mojo Town Orphanage. Bart followed them, carrying a large rucksack. He didn't really mind being the pack-mule; Sissy was getting too old and fat to carry much, and she puffed and wheezed like a sick bison as she struggled to get down the track without landing on her titanic posterior. And because of his gammy legs, Zak had to lean heavily on a walking stick to avoid slipping. Bart almost burst out laughing on more than one occasion.

The boy was also looking forward to seeing what was *really* down there. Although he was a curious child with an increasingly keen interest in scientic matters, Aunt Sissy and Uncle Zak had, from a very early age, filled all the children's heads with horror stories about the many monstrous things that thrived in the base of the crater.

"*Nevah* go down there by yerself," Aunt Sissy had told them. "Nasty critters will gobble ya up faster'n lightning. They like plump, juicy young'uns with nice crunchy bones especially!" She lifted her clawlike fingers and cackled insanely, scaring the heebie-jeebies out of the kids, Bart included.

Thus, he had avoided the crater … until now.

Not much grew in the sides of the crater—just moss, a few mangy tufts of grass, and some stunted-looking cacti. But the base of the hole was filled with some sort of dense vegetation, the same brilliant green as the tendrils that had sprouted from the backs of Holly and Ivy … and the Stuff in the jar. Even though it was still tucked in the slowly-shrinking shadow from the crater's eastern side, it almost seemed to glow.

Zak slid a few steps, and managed to jam the base of his cane into the rocks to avoid falling. "Watch yer step, Sissy, we's comin' to that real treacherous part."

"I knows it," Sissy huffed.

Carefully they continued down the narrow trail, now barely wide enough to move along sideways. The green resolved itself into a huge mass of tendrils. The pseudopods at the very centre of the mass were very long, soaring to many feet in the air, with smaller ones at the periphery. They were all shapes and sizes: some like whipcords, others thicker and shorter. Many were covered with warty growths. Some had mouths filled with sharp, uneven teeth that snapped at bugs and birds. A few had leaves and thorns, almost like normal plants. They all shifted and writhed gently of their own accord, creating a noise like leaves rustling in the wind. And, as Bart watched, they actually began to change shape. The long ones shortened, the fat ones thinned, the warty ones smoothed out, the mouths disappeared. It was eerily hypnotic.

Bart experienced a brief flare of horror as he recalled some of Sissy's stories, but curiosity soon clambered on top. What kind of flora … *fauna* was this? It seemed like the very essence of chaos itself.

"Nearly at tha bottom now, Sis!" Zak called as he struggled down the last few feet onto flatter ground. He paused to mop his forehead and catch his breath.

A frill-necked lizard, larger and with more legs than any self-re-specting lizard should have had, reared up on two pairs of hind limbs and hissed at Zak. It flicked out a tongue with multiple forks, spitting some sort of liquid at him.

"Damn critter!" Zak cursed, darting unsteadily to one side and man-aging to avoid the substance. It hit the ground, hissing and smoking like acid. He swung his cane, which was shod with iron, smashing the creature's head in. Its brains sprayed out across the rock. They were the same bright green as the tentacles. Its blood was a deep maroon in colour. "Drinkin' up all our Stuff!"

Sissy finally managed to get her enormous bulk down the rest of the trail. Bart jumped down nimbly behind her. "Neva mind tha blasted lizard, Zak. We's got work ta do!"

Zak pointed his cane at the ground, where the rocks gave way to a hole filled with bright green liquid. All the larger tendrils were grow-ing from it. "There it is. Whatever *it* is."

Sissy smiled, baring her uneven, fanglike teeth. "Amazing stuff, this. A magic pool just fer us ta make money outta."

She stood and marvelled at the writhing green shoots sprouting from the reservoir and swaying rhythmically in the wind. "Now let's git what we came fer. Hand me tha bucket," she commanded Bart as he unshouldered the pack, dumping it on the ground.

Bart unpacked the gear and laid it on the ground. The bucket con-tained several specimen jars, which he removed.

Sissy rolled up the legs of her dungarees, picked up the pail, and waded straight into the green liquid. The fluid rippled, thicker than water, more like syrup in its consistency. The small, ever-changing fronds curled around her bare, varicose-vein-covered legs. She dipped the bucket into the liquid and filled it.

Zak hung back at a safe distance with Bart. "Sissy, I dunno how you can just march in there barefoot. You shoulda brung some galoshes."

"It's *fine*, Zak." Sissy waded out with the slopping bucket. "Open and line up them jars, Bart."

Bart set to work.

"It's what's givin' yer them weird growths," Zak insisted.

Sissy hefted the bucket and started pouring the green Stuff into the bottles. "Fiddlesticks, Zak. I'm far too old for it ta do anythin' to me now. It only affects the littl'uns." She paused and looked hard at Bart, who was still lining up the jars. "Well, most of 'em, at least," she muttered. "No idea why you're still so ordinary and boring-lookin'." She went back into the liquid to collect another bucketful.

"Only the littl'uns? What about Ma and Pa?"

Sissy heaved an exasperated sigh. "We hadda put it in their juice for *weeks* before anythin' happened to 'em. I ain't been eatin' it at all. Now stop flappin' ya gums an' bein' such an idjit!"

Once the jars had been filled and their lids screwed back on good and tight, Sissy lifted one up and marvelled at how it shimmered in the mid-morning light. "Behold the Stuff dreams are made of—it heals, it grows, it mutates…!" She giggled. "Awright, that's enough standin' around jawing. Let's git back to the house fer lunch. I, fer one, am starving!" She motioned for Bart to stuff the bucket and jars back into the pack.

While she was struggling back up the last steep part of the cliff—with Zak behind her, believing he was helping by prodding her humungous backside with his cane—Bart paused before stuffing the last canister into his pack. He pulled a little flask from one pocket of his voluminous shorts and unstoppered it. Carefully, he poured a small quantity of the Stuff into his vial.

Sissy managed to scramble up onto the ledge with a loud gasp. She turned to see Bart putting the last jar into his pack. "Hurry up, slow-coach!" she shouted at him. "You don't want us ta leave ya here! Those plants look peaceful now, but they git mighty hungry after dark!"

"No, Aunt Sissy!" Bart shouldered the pack and hurried over.

* * *

Meanwhile, back at the orphanage, a moth fluttered in through the conservatory's open window, looking for somewhere to lay its eggs. It was quite large, with a wingspan of almost five inches. Strange markings on its thorax resembled a human skull, and it had a brightly-coloured abdomen. It bumbled around the room for a few minutes, and then landed on one of Pa's branches. The huge plant creature didn't notice the bug as he grumbled and muttered to Ma.

Realising it had found what it needed, the moth laid several clusters of eggs beneath the old human/plant hybrids' leaves. Then, its job done, it flew off to find a secluded corner to lie down and die in.

The eggs hatched a few days later, and tiny caterpillars, green, yellow, and brown in colour, wriggled out to take their first bites of the mutants' lush green leaves. As the baby caterpillars nibbled on Ma and Pa, absorbing the Stuff flowing through their bodies, they started to mutate as well. They grew rapidly into massive voracious monsters. After devouring all the leaves from the branches, they began on the new fruit that had just started to ripen.

Pa finally noticed the caterpillars, each now several feet long. "Dang it! There's creepy-crawly critters gnawin' on my love apples!"

Ma squealed in horror. Pa managed to snare a caterpillar with his vine-tongue and swallow it, and Ma used her long tongue to knock another from her trunk, but because of the Stuff, the larvae were more intelligent than normal. They quickly learned how to avoid Ma and Pa's only weapons. Connected to the walls by their branches and to the floor by their trunks, Ma and Pa could only move their necks and heads. They tried their hardest, but the hungry, hungry caterpillars managed to crawl onto their trunks, where their bark slowly merged back into flesh. They didn't like the hard, tough bark, but soon developed a taste for the softer human skin.

While Ma and Pa alternated between howling in agony and bellowing for help, the monstrous caterpillars began to eat their way up their bodies.

"Gag! I'm a goner, Ma!" Pa croaked.

Unfortunately, the conservatory was located on the top floor of an immense and rambling old house. Directly below lay a level that was only used by Sissy and Zak in the evenings; it contained their bedrooms, bathroom, and storage areas. And by the time the siblings retired for bed that particular night, nicely toasted on some elderberry wine, the caterpillars had already eaten off Ma's face and feasted on Pa's head.

* * *

Aunt Sissy kept Bart busy rendering some of the Stuff they'd harvested into an edible form that could be put into the children's porridge and stew. In its raw form, it burned the mouth and tongue. But no matter how much she boiled it, or how many herbs she added, Sissy couldn't get rid of its distinctive 'mouldy Brussels sprouts mixed with old socks' flavour. Fortunately she'd brought up the brats to not complain, and all it took to make Bart behave was a few small, meaningless, but well-placed words of praise.

Finally Bart managed to retreat into the old library for a few minutes with an old medical textbook that had been written during the Vyking War. He was a good third of the way in when something landed on the warped wooden boards nearby with a loud thud.

Bart jumped and clapped a hand over his mouth to stifle a squeal. "Who's there?" he called, thinking that Nate had snuck up on him as a joke.

But Bart was alone in the dim, dusty room. Then he picked out something that hadn't been there before: a dead bird that must have fallen from the top of a bookcase. Because there were so many fowls living in the library, Bart was always finding their tiny corpses. Initially he'd buried them in the yard, but lately, as his scienic interest grew, he'd taken to cutting them open to see what they looked like inside.

But as he picked this one up, he decided against dissecting it. He'd read a couple of ornithology books, but wasn't sure what kind of specimen this one was. It was about as big as a pigeon and had pretty, brightly-coloured feathers and a long plumed tail.

Bart slid his other hand into his pocket, where he kept the vial of Stuff. It was warm from the heat of his body, but still a brilliant green in colour. It seemed to last indefinitely. He put the bird and the Stuff down on a bureau and rummaged through his other pockets for a syringe he'd managed to purloin during the past week. He drew it out and filled it with some Stuff. Carefully he injected the dead bird in its throat.

He waited, watching the corpse intently, but, unsurprisingly, nothing happened. The bird lay still and dead.

"*Bart! Where'n tarnation are you?*" Sissy shrieked from somewhere.

Bart rolled his eyes, sighed, and departed the library. "Coming, Aunt Sissy!"

Sissy was standing in the hallway, holding a dead chicken in one hand and a dead piglet in the other. "Go an' feed Ma and Pa. It's bin a week since they were last seen to!"

Bart gulped. "Y-yes, Aunt Sissy."

She held out the dead animals. "We bin so busy workin' with the Stuff we plum fergot about 'em! They must be starvin' up there!"

Gingerly, Bart took the animals and Sissy bustled off back into the kitchen. *Stop bein' so squeamish*, Bart told himself. *You just stuck a needle in a dead bird, fer pity's sake!* He wasn't too worried by the dead chicken—he'd seen heaps of those, but the little pig was cute. He couldn't see any marks on it. Perhaps it had died of natural causes.

Bart carried the dead critters all the way up to the conservatory. Ascending the landing, he sniffed the air. Something was wrong. Where was the scent of elderberries? In its place was a fetid, musky odour, like stale urine. Was it simply the fertiliser he could smell? Cautiously, he pushed open the door.

But even though Bart had seen some awful things during his young life, he'd never seen anything quite as horrific as this. Ma and Pa had all but been eaten by giant mutant caterpillars. The larvae had feasted on the hybrids' fleshy parts until only two badly-chewed trunks remained, surrounded by fallen branches and pieces of bark. Two of the caterpillars, now ten feet long, nosed through the detritus, looking for any last morsel they might have forgotten. The rest were already hanging from the ceiling in the form of giant chrysalises.

The larvae lifted their heads as though sniffing the air. Their mouths were only small compared to their massive size, but those sharp fangs were still several inches long. And with their enhanced olfactory senses, they'd detected the presence of fresh meat standing in the doorway.

Two caterpillars lunged towards Bart.

Bart shrieked and threw the dead chicken and piglet towards the monsters, as hard as he could. Then he slammed the door and bolted.

"*Giant caterpillars et Ma and Pa!*" he screamed as he raced down the stairs three at a time. "*Aunt Sissy, caterpillars et Ma and Pa!*"

On the landing below he ran smack-bang into Zak, who was coming out of the bathroom.

"What's all that gawdawful hollerin' about, boy?" Zak demanded.

"It's Ma 'n' Pa…" Bart pointed emphatically upstairs. Tears burned his eyes. Ma and Pa had been awful mutants, and Ma had eaten Fido, but they hadn't deserved such a hideous end.

Zak limped upstairs to the conservatory and witnessed the devastation. Too busy fighting over the chicken and the piglet, the caterpillars didn't notice him. Zak's black eyebrows lowered menacingly. "Those low-down dirty mutant varmints et mah *parents!*"

Zak snatched up the pitchfork he used to spread the manure around and lunged at the squabbling monsters, impaling one through the head, pinning it to the wooden floorboards beneath with a loud thud. It thrashed and writhed in its death throes. The other lunged at him, closing its mouth around his leg.

"Uncle Zak!" Bart cried, looking wildly around for something else to attack with.

The caterpillar yanked on Zak's leg and he fell to the floor with a crash. He didn't look like he was in any pain, but swore at the monster, punching and slapping at it with his bare hands.

Bart noticed a shovel lying near the door and raced for it. He swung at the larva that was dragging Zak into the middle of Ma and Pa's remains.

"Leggo me leg, you ornery maggot!" Zak shouted.

Bart's shovel cut deep into the caterpillar's side, and thick dark blood squirted out. The infuriated creature released Zak and lunged at Bart. Bart swung at it again, but missed. He leapt backwards, skidded, and landed on his backside in the branches, bark, and chicken shit.

The huge monster reared over him to tear him to pieces—and then, suddenly, it crashed to the floor mere inches from him, dead.

Zak had grabbed the pitchfork from the other caterpillar and impaled it through the head of this one too. He straightened up, gasping for breath. "That was a close one!"

"Thank you, Uncle Zak!" Bart gasped.

Zak wagged a finger at him. "Now don't you git all soppy on me, Barton. I only saved ya coz ya too damn useful. Now come an' help me clean this mess up." He lurched from the room. His trouser leg was ripped from the larva's sharp teeth, but the boy couldn't see any blood on the cloth.

Bart climbed shakily to his feet. "Yes, Uncle Zak."

Zak got Bart to fetch the ladder, climb up, and saw down all the chrysalises. As they thudded onto the floor, Zak smashed them with a sledgehammer, bludgeoning them into bloody sludge. "Take *that*, you revoltin' bastards!"

Now the danger was over, Bart's curiosity returned. He wondered what would have come out of those gigantic cocoons. Now he'd never know. As Zak smashed up the last one, Bart caught a brief glimpse of markings that looked like a giant screaming skull.

Zak and Bart swept up all the remains of the caterpillars into burlap sacks and lugged them downstairs. They piled them up outside behind the barn and poured quicklime over them.

Zak straightened up with a groan. "That oughta dispose of them nasty buggers."

CHAPTER 8

After dinner that evening, Bart finished his chores and considered just retiring to bed because frankly, after the day's chaotic events, he was exhausted. But then he remembered the dead bird in the library. Had anything happened to it during the hours he'd spent cleaning up with Zak upstairs? Did the Stuff have any effect on lifeless flesh?

Taking a lamp, he crept into the library and over to the bureau where he'd left the bird, his needle, and the vial of Stuff. The fowl was still lying there, and at first he thought his experiment had failed. But then one of the bird's wings twitched slightly. Slowly it opened its beak, like a tiny baby taking its first cry.

Bart left the lamp beside it and raced out to fetch Nate, who was still helping to clean up in the dining room.

"You've gotta come and see this, Nate!" Bart cried, grabbing the smaller boy by the hand.

"What, what?" Nate gasped.

Bart pulled him across the hall into the library.

When they stepped into the gloomy room, something shot from the darkness, flying right at them! Both boys gasped and ducked. The bird Bart had injected soared away from them and headed for one of the windows. A strange, strangled screeching noise came from its throat.

"That's one angry bird!" Nate cried.

"It was dead, so I injected it with the Stuff, the green Stuff," said Bart as he hurried across the room towards it. The bird flew at the window, bashing against it with bone-breaking force. Furiously flapping its wings, it scrabbled against the glass with its beak and talons, trying to claw its way out.

"You *what*?" gasped Nate.

"I wanted to see what would happen! So far Aunt Sissy's only been usin' it on us, and we're livin' beings."

Nate grabbed Bart by an arm. "I'm scared!"

"Don't worry, I'll get it."

The bird fluttered jerkily from the window, as though drunk. It continued to make that awful screeching noise. Other birds in the library, who'd just settled down to rest, sprang from their roosts and fluttered into the air in terror, sending dust, feathers, and cobwebs flying everywhere. A few managed to leave the room through various cracks in the walls, but Bart's zombie bird didn't appear to be that smart; it continued to fly at the windows. Bart leapt into the air and tried to grab it, but it shot from his hands and launched itself with impressive speed at another pane.

This time the bird hit the glass so hard it smashed right through it. Through the shattered fragments and flying feathers, Bart and Nate caught a brief glimpse of the fowl as it dropped out of sight.

"Come on!" Bart raced from the library and out of the house into the cool, clear night. In the long grass beneath that particular window, Bart found the bird. It had sliced itself to ribbons flying through the broken window, and flopped limply in the boy's hands, dripping blood from numerous gashes. Once again it was dead.

"Whatta you gonna do?" asked Nate. "Bury it?"

"No, I gotta study it—find out what the Stuff really did to it."

Bart headed back to the library, and as they entered the room they noticed one of the other kids was inside, examining a dusty old book.

"Aw, no," said Nate before he could stop himself.

The girl looked up from the volume in her infant-sized hands. She had a beautiful rosy-cheeked face, with bright blue eyes and long silky blonde hair worn in two neat braids tied up with red ribbons. Her long, thin, sinuous snake body was dressed in a small blouse with puffy sleeves and a pleated plaid skirt lower down, where her hips would have been had she still possessed a human body.

But Anna now had the body of a snake, and when her legs fused, she'd learned to slither around like one. She could now move with all the grace and speed of a serpent, and brightly-coloured scales were starting to grow along her spine and spread down her ribs. Her little arms shrank daily and would probably merge with her body, one day soon. She was thirteen years old, and Sissy had already finished the treatment on her.

"Whatcha got there, Bart?" Anna asked silkily as she slid the book back into the shelf and glided up to him.

Bart whipped the dead bird behind his back. Blood continued to patter onto the floor. "Nuthin' that'ud int'rest you."

Anna rose up on her body, making herself taller than Bart. "It might."

"Since when have you bin int'rested in books, anyways?" Bart demanded.

Anna drew herself up even higher. "You think yer the only one here who knows howta read 'n' write? You think yer so smart? I kin read too, and I happen ta be very interested in snakes, considerin' what I'm becomin'. Fer example, did you know snakes can do this?" She opened her lower jaw and let it droop, making her mouth appear comically large.

"Bwaaaa?" said Bart, horrified by the sight. Her mouth was now big enough to wrap around his head.

She shook her head, clicking her jaw back in. "I learned howta do that the other day. Snakes need big mouths coz they swallow their food whole. I also happen to like magic tricks and cards, although it's becomin' a little hard for me to shuffle a deck." Anna wiggled her little fingers. Then, quick as the serpent she was, she darted over to the bureau and snatched up the small vial of Stuff. "What's this, then?"

"Just some green dye I was muckin' around with."

Anna reared up again. "Oh, fiddlesticks, Bart! I toldja before, I ain't stupid! It's some of Aunt Sissy's Stuff, and *ya not s'posed to have it.*"

"Um," said Bart, and he looked at Nate for help.

Nate shrugged.

"Shame on you, Barton, turnin' to that li'l baby!" Then, suddenly, she changed her tone. "Don't worry, I won't tell. I wanna help." And with that enigmatic little comment, she slithered away. As she passed the boys, she smiled at them and flickered her tongue at them. It was quite long and forked, just like a snake's.

Bart and Nate exchanged worried glances.

"I don't trust her," Nate whispered.

Bart nodded solemnly. "I don't either." He looked down at the mangled bird he was still clutching. He didn't feel like dissecting it now, and put it back on the bureau. It would keep until tomorrow. "C'mon, Nate—let's go to bed."

* * *

The orphans of Mojo County all occupied the first floor of the building. The older kids shared a large dormitory-sized room filled with bunk beds, while the little ones and their minders slept in smaller chambers. Bart and Nate occupied one of these rooms, and it overlooked the junkyard.

It was barely enough for one person, but two rickety old metal-framed beds, found in the junkyard, had been crammed in. The boys kept their clothes and other belongings on various shelves that lined the walls.

When Aunt Sissy had found Nate on the doorstep, she'd almost immediately passed him to Bart to take care of, to rock and feed and change. Even though the Stuff Aunt Sissy had injected directly into his pituitary gland had accelerated his growth, at a year old he was still considered an infant.

This suited the boys fine. Neither of them wanted to be transferred into the big room, where things could get a little rough.

Suddenly the bedroom door flew in with a crash, and Aunt Sissy appeared in the doorway, looking thunderous with her bony hands embedded in her well-padded hips. A long sinewy shape lurked in the hall behind her.

"Uh oh!" Nate darted under his covers.

"What's this I hear about you pinchin' some of my Stuff?" Aunt Sissy reached into the room and grabbed Bart by the front of his shirt, yanking him towards her.

"It—it was just a tiny little bit," Bart began, but couldn't finish because Aunt Sissy was shaking him so hard his head became a blur. "It's a tough job goin' down inter the crater to collect it, and you waste it on stoopid *birds*?" She stopped shaking him and he slumped in her grasp, dizzy and sick.

Anna smirked at him. Then she screwed up her face and poked her forked tongue at him. It flickered as she blew a very loud raspberry.

Sissy shoved Bart from her, and he flopped onto his bed. "Well, if yer so keen on usin' it for childish little experiments, from now on you ken climb down into the crater and fetch it all by *yerself*."

"But ... but what about ... all the critters?" Bart gasped.

"Zak's got an old cavalry sabre you ken borrow to fight 'em off." With that, Sissy turned and stomped off. Still flickering her tongue,

Anna slithered after her.

Bart swore and kicked the door shut.

Nate poked his head out from under the covers. "I *tol'ya* she couldn't be trusted!"

Bart sighed. "It ain't her fault. She can't help being a snake—it's become her nature. She is what she is now. Sneaky and treacherous."

The bedroom door creaked inwards and Anna slithered in. She flicked the door closed behind her with the tip of her tail. "See? I told ya I'd help!"

Even little Nate thought her answer was stupid. "Help? How is tellin' on us *helping*?"

Anna smiled. "Cause they trust me now, silly baby! I'm really on your side, you know that, don't cha?"

Bart stared intently at her. "Oh, suuuuuure."

CHAPTER 9

The next morning, Sissy stood in her dim, mouldy bathroom, dressed in her enormous corset and giant patched bloomers. She grimaced at her wrinkled complexion, once again wondering how such a magnificent beauty as hers had aged into such a hideous creature. She used to be so youthful and gorgeous, with many suitors clamouring for her hand. Of course, she'd refused them all, not wanting to be tied down at such a tender age. Like so many proud young lovelies, she'd assumed her appearance would stay with her.

Unfortunately, it hadn't, and the men had disappeared. When she was forced to fend for herself, her intelligence and her brother's knack for dodgy scams had enabled her to survive and even thrive. But where was she now? In a rundown dump, saddled with two dozen unwanted brats!

Hopefully their latest scheme would work and make them rich.

Sissy's growths had returned and were larger than before, longer and more twisted, bulging with warty lumps. "All right, Bart, your job is to cut off the ones I can't reach," she explained to the wide-eyed, horrified boy standing behind her. Slowly she undid the corset, revealing the ones sprouting from her back. "I can't rely on Zak to help me to do 'em—his eyes ain't what they useta be, and he refuses ta wear glasses, tha stoopid old fart. Think they make 'im look old or some such rubbish." She handed the boy a scalpel. "Watch the blade—it's sharp!"

Bart took it. He curled his fingers around it. All it would take was a single slash to her thick neck, and the old witch would be slumped to the floor in a puddle of blood. He would be free. His hand shook. Could he do it?

"Come on now, boy, what'choo waitin' fer? All yer gotta do is cut 'em off. I heal fast—no need to worry about the blood. You seen worse downstairs." She reached around behind her to a thick, knotty growth, and wiggled it with her fingers. It twitched like a worm on the hook.

Bart took the repulsive thing in one hand and lifted the scalpel, raising it behind Sissy's back so it was level with her throat. He could see her carotid artery pulsing. It would be *so damn easy* to slash it. His heart started to race with excitement as he realised he held Sissy's life in his hands. What would Zak do if he killed her? Stumble after him on his bum legs?

He couldn't believe that she trusted him. No, he realised, she didn't trust him at all. She just assumed he'd never even think of doing such a thing.

But he would. Just now wasn't the right time.

Bart blinked and cut off the tumour. Unfortunately, he cut too close to Sissy's body, and she yelped in pain. "Ouch, ya stoopid little bastard! That was *me* you cut, not the damn wart!"

"Sorry, Aunt Sissy! Won't happen again! I know what I'm doin' now!" He grabbed a cloth and pressed it against the bleeding cut, holding it in place until the blood clotted. Then he reached for another gnarly tendril near Sissy's waist. He noticed that she had a nasty, badly-stitched scar running around her middle, almost like she'd been cut in half and sewn back together or something. He ran a finger along it, wondering what it was and how she got it.

"What'choo doin' there, boy?" she demanded. "Stop yer dawdlin'! I 'aven't got all day!"

But before he could apologise for being inappropriate, someone knocked at the front door. The only reason they heard it was because speaking tubes connected the ground floor rooms to those on the second floor.

"Hell's bells!" Sissy bellowed. "Who in tarnation could that be at this hour? Zak, *ZAK*!"

Zak didn't answer.

Sissy heaved a huge sigh. "Dang fool! What's the bet he's still lyin' in bed! Hafta do ever'thing my damn self. Gimme my gown, boy."

Bart snatched up Sissy's voluminous pink dressing gown and held it open so she could slip into it. He heaved a huge sigh of relief when her massive wrinkly bulk was mercifully concealed once more.

She clomped downstairs and along the hall to the front door. She yanked it open to the sight of a tall, thin, rather sad-looking woman with long blonde hair that fell limply over her shoulders without any adherence to style. It framed a sallow face with hollow cheeks and shadowed blue eyes. She was dressed in a plain dark-blue gown and a shapeless woollen cardigan. She looked like she'd just come out of hospital or a sanatorium.

Expecting to see yet another single mother about to deposit a baby, Sissy drew herself up, making sure that her robe was closed, and that she had a suitably friendly expression on her face. "Can I help you?"

The woman gulped and fiddled with the buttons on her jacket. "Um … my name is Louisa Bigelow," she said softly. "I left my baby Nathaniel here a year ago. I've … I've come to take him home."

Sissy raised an eyebrow. She couldn't remember the last time any of Mojo Town's inhabitants had actually wanted one of their own back.

She stepped aside. "Please come inside."

She took Louisa into a little-used parlour at the front of the house, where she invited the lady to sit on a dusty old couch. She returned a few minutes later with some tea and biscuits.

"I hit rock bottom," Louisa explained. "I was dreadfully sick, and I woulda died had a kind friend not looked in on me an' found me unconscious in bed. He took me to hospital and paid for my recovery." She bowed her head, her long stringy hair obscuring her face. "I'm livin' in a nice apartment in Bhigge Smoche now, and I'm ready to take mah boy and give 'im the life he deserves."

Sissy reached out and gave Louisa what she hoped was a reassuring pat on the hand. "I'm so sorry, dearie, but we didn't find yer poor wee lad till morning. In the cold and rain he musta caught a chill. The doctor did all he could, but I'm afraid he died. He's buried in the cemetery next door. He's sleeping peacefully now."

Louisa gaped at Sissy in horror. Then the rest of the colour drained from her face. "No," she croaked. "No, no, no!" She burst into tears.

Sissy slipped an arm around Louisa's narrow shoulders and cuddled her close to her enormous bosom. "There, there, dearie. It's bin a tryin' time fer all of us here. My own sweet, sweet parents passed away just last week."

Louisa continued to cry, but managed through her tears to say: "I … I'm so sorry to hear that."

"Yar, it was most unexpected," Sissy continued. "Still in the full bloom of their lives, living a lush and fruitful existence…" She passed Louisa a handkerchief and she blew her nose.

"Thank you," Louisa whispered. "I'm wondering—could you show me where my poor Nathaniel's buried?"

"I'd take you meself, but as you can see I'm not dressed yet! But ya can't miss his resting place. It's under a big ol' oak tree."

"Of course—thank you very much for your help. I'm so sorry to have bothered you so early." Despondently, Louisa left the room.

* * *

Louisa was too wrapped in her grief to notice Bart crouched in the hall beside the parlour door, using a scratched-up side table as cover while he eavesdropped on the whole conversation. Unfortunately Zak, lurching from the dining room, spotted the boy immediately.

"Ya little sneak!" He grabbed the boy by an ear and dragged him into the parlour where Sissy was still seated, enjoying the tea and biscuits.

"Caught this young whippersnapper listenin' in. What d'ya wanna do ta him? Give 'im a thrashing, teach 'im a lesson?"

Bart struggled to squirm from the cruel tight grip on his ear. Zak gave him a crow's peck on the top of his head, then let him go.

Bart yelped in pain, clapping his hands to his head.

Sissy rose to her feet. "Quit foolin' around, you pair. There's work ta be done!"

Bart turned to dart from the room.

"And where d'ya think you're going, young man?" Sissy demanded, hands on hips.

"Uh, to ah, do work?"

"That can wait," Sissy growled. "There's still the question of your punishment."

Bart lifted his hands. "Punishment? But I didn't hear anything!"

"Maybe you did, maybe you didn't. You still deserve ta be punished. You left the conservatory winda open, so it's *your* fault that Ma and Pa got et by them 'pillas."

Bart could only stare in horror. "Huh? But you tol' me to—"

Sissy swept a hand across her body. "No buts! It don't matter what I tol' ya. You did it, so you're ta blame. You hafta be punished."

Bart balled his hands into fists. "That's not fair!"

"*Life's* not fair. Life's wot ya' make of it. An' so far, you ain't made much of yours." She caught hold of one of Bart's skinny little wrists and squeezed hard. He cried out in pain again.

"Look atcha!" She shook the hand she held. "Even the Stuff don't take to ya. It ain't easy goin' down inta that blasted crater ta fetch it, an' it's wasted on you!" She held up his hand, examining it more closely. He had a sixth finger growing next to his pinky. "*No one's* gonna pay ta see this! Every second inbred yokel's got an extra didjit!"

Bart struggled to pull his arm free, but Sissy had an even stronger grip than Zak's. And she was in full rant now, so he had no chance of escaping.

"The only reason yer still here an' not down in the boneyard is coz yer a hard worker and there's *plenny* o' chores ta be done 'round here. Gotta earn yer keep somehow. Now what's yer punishment gonna be, hmm? No supper for a fortnight? Maybe a whippin' like Zak suggested?"

Bart continued to wriggle. "That ain't right!"

"Don't you sass me, boy! I'm your elder and that means I'm *always* right. You need ta learn ta respect yer elders!"

Bart realised he couldn't win against such unfair illogic. He hung his head and fumed. He wished he had cut Sissy's throat when he'd had the chance.

"Answer me, boy, what's yer punishment gonna be, then?"

"Dunno," Bart muttered into his chest. A hundred smart-mouthed answers raced across his brain, but he knew all of them would be met with more pain and derision.

"Not much yer do know, is there?" Sissy demanded.

Not much I know? Bart thought. *Yar, right! If I was so dumb you wouldn't get me to help with your experiments, would you? You picked me because you* know *I'm smart, but you just won't admit it.* He kept this knowledge boiling deep inside the pit of his gut, a burning flame he could cling to.

"Hard worker you might be, but you ain't too bright between the ears." Sissy knocked on his head again.

Bart had had enough of people rapping on his head like it was the front door. As she lifted his hand to strike him again, he pulled away with the reflexes of a cat.

Sissy stepped back, momentarily surprised by the lightning speed of his reflexes. Then she relaxed and cackled wickedly. "You're mighty quick there, boy. I reckon you can handle a lot more chores and do 'em a lot quicker than we firs' thought. What ya reckon about that, eh? We'll start with that. Let's see how good you do yer chores and I might spare ya the rod. Now, that's a fair deal. Ain't it?"

Bart managed a nod. "Yes, Aunt Sissy."

"Now I need some firewood chopped up. The lads from down the road just brung up a fresh haul."

"But—" Bart caught himself upon seeing the fierce look that Sissy gave him. He gulped. "Yes, Aunt Sissy."

Bart took a deep breath, counted to ten inside his head, then turned and skulked out of the room.

When he was gone, Zak—who'd been quiet the whole time, simply watching with a sardonic look on his face—cleared his throat. "Sooo—who was that lady, anyway? She was a bit pale an' skinny, but still quite a looker!" He licked his lips.

Sissy glared at him, but lowered her voice conspiratorially: "That was Nate's nosy mother snooping about lookin' for 'im. I convinced her the kid's dead."

Zak grinned. "You always seem ta know the right thing ta say, Sissy."

After her harrowing morning, Sissy refused to be mollified. "Some-one's gotta be the brains of this outfit. Now, are you all set? I need you to collect enough critters tonight for tomorrow's operation."

Zak actually flicked off an enthusiastic salute: "Righto, Sissy."

Sissy smoothed down her dressing gown. "Now I'd better go'n check on our little darlings. Make sure they ain't killed each other durin' the night or some other such stupidity."

* * *

Bart muttered and grumbled to himself on his way outside to the woodpile. Again he thought about holding that scalpel to Sissy's throat. He focussed on how he'd felt, holding her life in his hands. Slowly he calmed down. He hadn't blustered or threatened, so he figured she'd ask him to do that again. She thought she was humiliating him, but really she was giving him power over her. She didn't realise that he would cut her throat if and when he felt the time was right.

His heart slowed and his body temperature fell. He mopped his brown curls from his eyes and straightened up. Chores weren't a problem. Chores he could handle. They enabled him to exercise and focus his mind on the tasks at hand. When he exerted himself, his thoughts simplified; they ceased chasing their tails in endless circles around his mind. He could solve one problem at a time.

As he approached the pile, he noticed a new, very sharp axe leaning against the heap. He picked it up, hefting it in his hands. He imagined driving it through Sissy's body. Why would she even leave something like this lying around? He could easily waltz into the house with it before she or Zak knew about it. And by the time he'd hacked Sissy to death, that crippled, unsteady brother of hers wouldn't be able to stop him.

He tightened his grip. Now he had the strength to stay the distance. He had to keep plodding along, doing what he was told, and learning what he could along the way. For Nate's sake.

Bart noticed something bright lying in the shadow of the woodpile, and picked up a crayon one of the younger kids must have left lying around. This child had scribbled some crude cartoons on one of the logs.

He slipped it into one pocket of his baggy shorts.

CHAPTER 10

Adjusting her blouse and skirt, Sissy lumbered up the steep creaking stairs to the children's dorms on the first floor. The worn old treads creaked ominously beneath her weight. "Now let's just see how my little pretties are farin'," she muttered to herself.

She stomped across the landing and unlocked the door to the main dormitory where most of the young'uns lived. She kept them locked in during the nighttime. She didn't trust them not to wander during that period. In the early days, she hadn't bothered to keep them shut in, and consequently lost a few to the junkyard and crater, where they'd succumbed to accidents and local critters. A couple had wandered off and disappeared completely—she had no idea what had become of them. But she didn't think they'd gone to the sheriff; otherwise, she would have received a visit by now.

These days some deaths occurred because the children fought between themselves, but most who died now did so because of her awful experiments.

Sissy didn't particularly want them to fight—she lost good material that way. But neither did she want to hear about their silly childish problems, such as who pissed in whose bed, who stole whose clothes, and who pulled whose hair/tentacles/other appendages. She only wanted to hear gossip if it affected her directly, like when Anna told her Bart had taken some of the Stuff.

Sissy pushed the door inwards, and immediately the chaos within righted itself. The kids scrambled to clean up and dress. She'd arranged for them to have a bathroom of their own so they didn't have to worry about emptying overflowing potties.

"Awright now, line up!" she bellowed in her best Constitutional Army parade-ground voice. "Let's see how yer doin', then!"

Her mutant children shuffled from their various beds, desks, and play areas to assemble in a ragged line in front of her. She sniffed disdainfully at their lack of discipline. "Please try ta be quicker next time. I don't have all day ta wait for you ta prance around prettyin' yerselves up." She started to walk along the line, examining them.

At the beginning of the line stood the twins Holly and Ivy, back to back. Both were looking particularly bad-tempered and surly, standing with their arms folded and pouting disdainfully. But the stitch-marks from their joining were now almost invisible. Sissy ran a long, bony finger along the line. "Oh yes, the scars are disappearin' nicely. It won't be long now, and you'll look like proper Siamese twins. All you hafta do now is learn howta move in unison."

The girls looked up at Sissy in confusion.

Sissy planted her hands on her hips. "If you wanna be true Siamese twins, you gotta learn howta move *tagether*! If you bin like that since ya bin born, you should already know howta *git around*!" She clapped her hands. "C'mon now! I showed you some moves. One of youse has gotta take the lead."

Holly and Ivy twisted their heads and exchanged glances. Both lowered their eyebrows menacingly.

"One of youse is the leader!" Sissy shouted. "Otherwise you'll *nevah* be convincin'!"

Ivy sighed and bowed her head, conceding defeat to her more dominant sister. Holly nodded. "All right, Aunt Sissy."

"Knew'd you get it! Now keep practisin' what I taught ya!" She moved along to the next child, the one with multiple eyes in his head and two sets of arms sprouting from his elbows. He also had two sets of legs coming from his knees, and could only scuttle about on all fours—or rather, all eights. Sissy made him run back and forth, making sure he could move fluidly, as though he'd been born with his deformity. "And how are you today, Spider Boy?" she asked with deceptive kindness.

He looked up at her, blinking through his numerous eyes. His spidery mandibles ensured that he could no longer speak normally. He clacked them at her, and she took that to mean approval, even though it was actually a swear word.

Sissy moved along the line of kids to one who was wearing a large ceramic jar around his middle. His arms protruded from holes at the sides, and his legs from the base. He was one of her first experiments, based on research she'd done from documents she had procured. This was by far her oldest child, but the jar she'd forced him into at an earlier age ensured that he was no bigger than any of the other pubescent kids. Only his head, hands, and feet were the size they should have been, and appeared comically large emerging from such a spindly creature.

"And how's my Jarboy coming along?" she purred.

He scowled at her.

"Good job!" She pinched one of his cheeks, and then moved along to the next freak: a girl with a normal body, but seven heads sprouting from her shoulders. All wore their hair in braids tied up with bows. "Ah, look! Here's Matilda, Margaret, Minnie, Mabel, Marjorie, Maisey and Maude. My Gaggle Girls." Sissy clasped her hands together in delight. "All of the heads have taken!" She started firing questions at the girls, one by one, and they answered dutifully. "And you're all perfectly

intelligent! No dummies at all! Marvellous!"

Sissy came up to the obese boy with a giant mouth that extended all the way to his belly button. She got him to open that huge gob. A lot of sharp teeth appeared, all held together with a formidable set of braces. "Those'll come off tomorra, Balloon Boy," she promised him.

Then Sissy came to Anna, who was swaying gently back and forth. Out of all the children, she appeared the happiest, the least resentful of what had been done to her. Her hair was also up in braids tied with bows. Because her arms were now so short, she couldn't style it anymore, and the Gaggles had done it for her. Her new scales glittered in the sunlight that filtered in through the dusty window. Her back was now completely covered with beautiful multi-coloured patterns.

Sissy was really impressed. "Ah, Python Girl. You're scaling up quite nicely."

Anna smiled sweetly at Sissy.

Sissy slipped a hand into a pocket of her skirt. "I have a little present for you, seeing's how you've bin such a good girl." She gave Anna a red lipstick.

"Thank you, Aunt Sissy!" Anna purred.

Sissy patted Anna on the head and left the room.

As soon as the door closed, the other kids crowded around her, glaring intimidatingly at her. "You slimy little suck-up!" growled Holly.

"Yeah," said Jarboy, waddling over and shaking an oversized fist. The others made various noises of agreement. Then Rex bit her on the tail.

Anna flicked the quadruped boy off, sending him sliding across the floor. She reared up until she was several feet taller than the tallest child, and hissed. "'Nuff of that, or I just might strangle one o' you stoopid bullies in yer sleep!" Suddenly her scales flashed, and started to change colour and pattern.

The angry kids tried to look away, but Anna's designs seemed to shift and change, never appearing the same way twice. They were strangely hypnotic and soothing. The children's rancour faded, and they dispersed back to their various areas.

"Oh, Sissy'll be sick of her soon enough," grumbled Matilda, one of the Gaggle Girls.

"Yeah, when she starts work on Nate, she'll fergit *all* about her," agreed Ivy.

Anna simply smiled, then opened her flexible jaw so she could apply the lipstick all the way around her enormous mouth. *Strangle* and *eat*, she thought to herself.

* * *

Sissy went next door to the little room to check on Nate. Since Bart was off doing his chores, Nate was busy plumping up the pillows and making the two narrow beds. He stopped and looked fearfully up at Aunt Sissy as she loomed in the doorway.

"And my little Nathaniel … What a fine strappin' young man you're growin' into," she purred. "No one would ever guess you were just a baby when you came here a year ago."

Sissy pushed her way into the room, in between the beds, and up to the window. Nate had to climb onto his bed to get out of her way. She opened the curtain a crack and peered out. Directly below, she could see Bart diligently chopping wood, just like she'd asked. He'd already produced an impressive pile. Looking further afield she could see Louisa crouched on top of the hill in the cemetery, where the big oak tree stood. Beneath lay a lot of small graves. Only Sissy knew who was buried in them.

She cackled to herself and let the curtain fall.

"What'choo laughin' at, Aunt Sissy?" Nate asked.

She looked down at him. "Oh, nothin' you need to worry your little head about, Nate." She ruffled his blond hair and left the room.

* * *

Once, many years earlier, when the old oak tree had been alive and thriving, it provided a popular spot for the locals of Mojo Town to bury their beloved. But when it died and started to rot, the townspeople left the site for paupers and orphaned children.

Now the old oak stood blackened and pitted, minus most of its branches save for a few gnarly limbs that looked more like monstrous claws. The headstones from long-forgotten townspeople were lopsided and faded, and some had been stolen to provide new stones for fresh graves elsewhere. The children's graves were marked with various makeshift headstones and crude wooden crosses. Some had names scratched onto them; others were bare.

Directly below the tree, Louisa knelt beside a tiny grave. It was marked with a piece of someone else's headstone, cracked from one of the older graves and jammed into the dirt. The name gouged into the headstone read "Nathaniel NoName".

"Oh, my poor little wine-stained boy," Louisa sobbed. "I finally got mah life together. I met a good man I intend ta marry. He woulda been a fine father to you. I'm sorry, Nathaniel. I tried to do my best for ya, but I guess it wasn't enough." She bowed her head, fresh sobs tearing through her frail, slender body.

* * *

As Bart chopped the firewood, a small flat piece splintered off. He paused, looked around to make sure no one was watching, and then used the crayon he'd pocketed to write a quick message on the smooth-cut side. Then he noticed the curtain of his bedroom window twitch aside and Sissy's old, wrinkled face look down at him. Tossing the fragment aside, he hefted the axe and went back to work, making sure to swing quickly and enthusiastically for her benefit. Occasionally he glanced up to see if she was still watching.

But she'd directed her attention to Louisa on the hill under the dead oak tree. When the curtain dropped, Bart snatched up his message, raced from the yard, and darted through the side gate into the cemetery. He dashed through the graves towards the hill, and when he thought he was close enough, he hurled the small plank of wood towards the children's graves.

* * *

Through her tears, Louisa heard something thud onto the ground behind her. She spun in horror, but only saw a fragment of wood lying in the long yellow grass. She assumed it had fallen from the tree. In her grief she didn't notice that it was fresh and clean, unlike the rotting oak. Miserably, she climbed to her feet, brushed down her long plain gown, and started to walk from the cemetery.

Bart crouched down behind a tall tombstone. Every nerve inside him screamed for him to race up to her and tell her what he'd written on his note. But he'd never spoken to anyone outside the orphanage, and fear froze him to the spot. His heart raced.

Louisa departed the cemetery and headed down the street to where a mechanical carriage was parked, its engine rumbling idly. Puffs of smoke emerged from its tall black chimney.

Run, Bart! Before she disappears! the boy screamed inside his mind. But he couldn't do it. He was too terrified. The lad who'd held a razor-sharp scalpel to Sissy's throat and thought about slashing her carotid artery, without any emotion whatsoever, couldn't bring himself to approach that sad, beautiful woman.

Louisa climbed into the carriage. The driver yanked on chain-reins, bringing the machine out of idle mode. With a rumble, it rolled off down Boneyard Way.

Bart slumped behind the gravestone. With a curse he thumped the stone repeatedly until his knuckles started to bleed. Then he climbed despondently to his feet and retrieved his message. He couldn't risk anyone else seeing it.

CHAPTER 11

Later that day, after dinner, Zak took Bart down into Mojo Town. Bart had no time to enjoy the unexpected outing, as he had to push a large wheelbarrow filled with hessian sacks. He also had no idea what they were about to do, and didn't dare ask Zak in case he rapped him over the head again. Zak had his cane in one hand and a bag of something in the other. He looked right and left as they skulked through the dusty back streets and alleys of the town's poorest area, located at the base of the hill that the orphanage dominated.

Here the houses were little more than tumbledown hovels built from whatever people could find lying around. At the western edge of the town stood the power station, which blanketed the area with thick black smoke day and night. But the electrical wires humming overhead bypassed the shanties, heading for the richer folks' dwellings further east, where the air was cleaner. One wire ran up the hill to the orphanage to provide power to Sissy's basement.

The workers slaved to keep the station running, but couldn't afford to reap its benefits. Still, they were paid for their efforts, and even a small wage was better than starving.

It was in this area that the town's stray cats congregated. Zak noticed a large ginger tom sitting atop one of the rickety back fences. "Here, puss-puss-puss", he crooned as he reached into the bag he'd brought with him, and brought out some leftover meat that was a little on the nose. "Have one o' them sacks ready, Bart," he told the boy.

With a sinking feeling in his stomach, Bart readied a bag. This wasn't going to end well.

Zak placed the food on the ground, and the hungry cat darted over to sniff it. He stroked the cat as it ate, and it purred in pleasure. Then he tightened his grip on the scruff of its neck, and before it could react, he stuffed it into one of the hessian sacks and twisted the bag closed. It meowed and struggled, claws ripping into the cloth. Zak dropped the bag on the ground and gave it a good hard whack with the steel end of his cane. The animal ceased its struggling.

"Wh-what's the cat for, Uncle Zak?" gasped Bart. "We don't need to feed Ma and Pa no more."

"It's a surprise. Now be quicker next time. Don't want too much racket ta get out and alert tha neighbours."

They continued along the street, and Bart noticed a pile of garbage up ahead. A shadowy shape was sniffing around in it, and he pointed it out.

Zak squinted. "Ah, good, well-spotted, Bart. Here, kitty-kitty-kitty." He put more meat down, and a black cat emerged to check out the free meal. Zak handed his cane to Bart and readied the bag. "Get ready ta give it a good hard smack soon as it's in the sack," he ordered.

Bart gulped. "B-but Uncle Zak—I don't wanna—"

Zak turned on him. "Do as ya damn well told, boy! I can't be expected to catch 'em *and* knock 'em out!"

Bart gulped again. He didn't want to beat poor defenceless cats to death, but it was either them or him. Miserably, he hefted the heavy cane.

As the black cat ate, Zak whipped the bag over its head and wrapped it up. "Hit it *now*!"

Bart gave it a half-hearted whack that didn't do much. The cat screeched in distress.

"*Agin!*" Zak snarled.

Bart smashed the cane down where he assumed the cat's head was. There was a sickening crunch as its skull shattered like a china cup, and it fell limp. His stomach lurched, and he swallowed repeatedly to keep his bile down. This wasn't killing chickens or pigs for food—this was like losing Fido all over again. Some of these poor felines could have been pets.

"Better," said Zak. "But don't wimp out on me agin. This is important."

"H-how many do we need?" asked Bart miserably.

"Half a dozen oughta do it."

It was easy to locate cats in this part of town, and they quickly collected three more. As the sun set, gaslights began to flare into life. Bart began to struggle to push the large barrow. Once a whine came from a feline that hadn't been completely knocked out, and Zak, who had his cane back to help him walk, gave it an enthusiastic smack that nearly tipped the whole lot out on the road.

Bart spotted a tabby cat perched up in a tree with its tail hanging down. Being tall and skinny, Zak managed to catch hold of the tail and yank the cat down, but it twisted in mid-air and swiped at his hand, opening several deep cuts. It lunged up into higher branches and hissed in fury. "Bloody hell!" Zak cursed. "Bart, it's the last one. Go up there an' git it!"

Bart scrambled up the tree and carefully made his way along the branch towards the furious feline. He reached out for the cat, but it snarled at him and leapt down.

It launched itself directly at Zak's face with its claws extended. Before Zak could bring up his arms to protect himself, the cat's talons raked down his nose, opening more gashes.

"Consarn it!" Zak snarled. Somehow he managed to catch hold of the furious animal and yank it from him. It snarled and kicked in his grip. "Yeow! Damn varmint! Bart, git the sack before the sonuvabitch claws me ta bits!"

Bart jumped down from the tree, nearly twisting an ankle in the process, and grabbed the bag.

"Get in there, ya mangy moggy!" Zak stuffed it in and then swung the bag with all his might at the trunk of the tree. There was a crunch as the feline's ribs caved in and its spine snapped. Bart winced, and his guts rolled again.

Gasping for breath, Zak tossed the bag in with the others. Bart could see thick dark blood dripping from his face onto his white shirt. "This is your fault, y'know!" Zak barked at him.

Bart gaped at Zak in horror. He couldn't believe his senses and had no idea how to respond. There was no right way. Why was he always in the wrong?

"Aw, shut yer trap and let's git this lot home!" Zak grabbed his cane and lurched off up the hill, towards the grim lonely sentinel way up on top. As they left the gaslights of the town, the rising moon became their only guiding light.

An elderly lady shuffled out onto her rickety old back stoop, cupped her hands around her mouth and called: "Here kitty-kitty-kitty! Where's that darn cat? Usually she comes when I call…"

* * *

Back at the orphanage, Sissy tended to Zak's numerous cat scratches. He whined every time she dabbed one with iodine. She bandaged his hands and put sticking plasters on his face. Bart did all he could to help, and then turned to leave so he could retire to bed.

"Yer ain't finished yet," Sissy snapped before he could leave.

Bart rolled his eyes and groaned. *What now?* he wondered in exasperation.

"Come on, you ain't finished what you were doin' this morning, before I was so rudely interrupted by that nosy blonde hag."

* * *

In her bathroom, Sissy had stripped back down to her corset and big bloomer underwear so Bart could finish slicing off the rest of her growths. He noticed that the ones he'd removed earlier had already healed, only tiny scars remaining. The Stuff had accelerated her regeneration. What else had it done to her?

Again he lifted the scalpel behind her, where she couldn't see it, and imagined whipping it across her throat. This time he almost did it. But at the last instant, he remembered the growths. Would her enhanced regeneration save her from bleeding to death?

He couldn't risk her surviving. He knew if she did, he wouldn't.

Sissy shivered and wrapped her bony arms around her shoulders. "Go'wan git some more wood fer tha fire. I'm gonna catch a chill standin' here in mah smalls."

Bart gripped the scalpel, gaping at her in horror.

"Don't just stand there mouthing like a fish! Whatta ya waitin' for? *Bring me some gordamn wood, boy!*"

Bart counted to ten inside his head as he stomped off. He brought up a load of freshly-cut firewood for the big stove in the bathroom. He thrust some logs in, along with the piece containing the message to Louisa.

He watched it burn.

* * *

The next morning, directly after breakfast, Sissy and Zak took Bart and Nathaniel down into the basement. Nathaniel, who'd never been down there before, baulked at being in the grim dark space with all the evil-looking specimens in jars. Some had eyes that were still open, and their dead, glassy stare seemed to follow him around the room. The unblinking electric light only made things look even more mysterious.

"Git me tools ready, Bart," Sissy ordered.

"Wh-what you gonna do with Nate?" asked Bart worriedly.

"Don't'choo worry about him, Bart. Just do as yer told," she growled at him, in a tone that didn't invite any further negotiation.

Bart, who was still exhausted from the previous day of activity, turned to fetch all the surgical instruments and line them up on the bench. He tried not to think about what was going to be done to Nate, but he had an incredibly active imagination.

Sissy got Nate to take off his shirt and lie down on his belly on the operating table. But as Zak tightened the leather straps around his arms and legs, Nate started to struggle. Then Sissy approached him with a needle.

Nate shrieked in terror at the sight of the evil-looking thing.

Bart gulped, torn in a hundred different directions. He grabbed a scalpel before he realised what he was doing. *No*, he told himself, and quickly put it back down. He couldn't try anything right now. Nate could end up an innocent victim. He knew that Sissy didn't want to kill. She wanted to create. She was, at heart, an artist. A homicidal artist, yes, but still an artist.

"Hold 'im still!" Sissy ordered Zak. She thrust the needle into his throat. Nate gave a gurgle of fear before his eyes glazed over and he slumped limply onto the table. Bart cringed.

"Good, good," Sissy approved. "Bart, git tha ether ready. But not too much. It don't grow on trees, ya know."

Bart drew the gas mask down over Nate's face, tying it securely, and turned the wheel on the gas bottle. He felt sick, his breakfast churning in his guts. He really didn't want to be a party to this operation. Nate was the closest thing he had to a friend.

"Zak, brother dear, I do hope you got enough cats for tha operation."

Zak drew himself up. "Plenny more where they came from, Sissy," he proclaimed with more confidence than he intended.

Sissy simply sniffed. "Well, start gettin' 'em ready. And be quick about it. We don't 'ave all day." She held out a hand. "Hand me a scalpel, Bart."

Bart felt like shoving it through her palm. Instead he gave it to her properly.

Zak hung up one of the dead cats by its back feet, pulled out a skinning knife, and set to work. He'd done this sort of thing before, and knew how to get the pelt off in one piece. "Why're we doin' this operation now, Sissy? Shouldn't we be waitin' till he's a bit older?"

"Injectin' the Stuff directly into his pituitary gland made 'im age a lot faster than normal, so I'm gonna take advantage of his fast growth while I can. Also, the quicker he's changed, the quicker he'll be unrecognisable in case that skinny blonde tramp comes back and starts sniffin' 'round." With the scalpel, Sissy cut some skin away from Nate's back, shoulders, buttocks, and thighs.

As Zak continued to skin the dead cats, Sissy ordered Bart to pass her a canister of the Stuff. Carefully she painted Nate's raw, exposed muscles with it.

Sissy took the first cat's skin and cut it into shape. She placed the raw pelt against Nate's back. The second one she fitted around his lower back and buttocks, with a strip of fur from the cat's tail hanging down at the base of his spine. The third and fourth she sliced into strips and grafted to his arms. The fifth and sixth she attached to the backs of his legs. The Stuff ensured they stuck straight away.

"Enough?" asked Zak. "Or should I git some more cats tonight?"

His eyes gleamed with excitement. He'd enjoyed catching and killing the town's strays, and he wanted payback for his cut hands and face.

Sissy rubbed her chin. "Naw. He's a little patchy now, but give 'im a few days and he'll smooth over and start lookin' more authentic. Mark my words." She directed her attention to Bart. "Now you ken clean up the lab and get rid of the dead cats. Feed 'em to the pigs or somethin'."

As Sissy disconnected Nate from the ether and Zak unstrapped him, Bart set to work, cleaning up the blood, washing the instruments, and taking the dead cats out to the pig pen. Deep down he was relieved. He didn't consider turning Nate into some sort of furry cat-child nearly as bad as what Sissy had done to some of the others, such as Spider Boy, the Gaggle Girls, and Holly and Ivy. At least he would still be roughly human, with one head, two arms and two legs.

But tears still coursed down Bart's cheeks as he worked. He wondered how much longer he'd be able to endure this life before he did something drastic. Even though he still looked normal on the outside, despite his extra fingers, changes were taking place inside him, and sometimes the strangest thoughts and ideas whirled around inside his head.

He was sure he would never have thought about killing Sissy in the past. Was he becoming just as big a monster as she?

CHAPTER 12

Nate came to later that day, but Bart couldn't tend to him until after dinner, when Sissy finally released him from his chores. He washed and staggered into their little bedroom, where Nate was sitting up in bed and looking at his arms. The cat fur had already taken, and the backs of both limbs were covered with thick, soft fur. The different colours were already merging, flowing together to become one uniform pattern. Even his blond hair had started to join with the fur on his back, and was becoming thicker and more golden.

He looked up as Bart stepped into the room and smiled, glad to see him. "It itches," he complained.

"That'll stop," Bart promised. "It's still settling in."

"So she's trynna turn me into some sorta cat?"

"I reckon so." Bart cupped Nate's face in his hands, looking closely at him. He made out more changes as the cats' various essences were being absorbed into Nate: pupils elongating into slits, ears rising towards the top of his head and growing points, small whiskers sprouting from his cheeks. "Open your mouth."

Nate did so. Already his teeth were growing pointier.

"Yar, you're turnin' into a cat boy, all right. But it's a dang sight better than a spider boy or snake girl. Can you see any different?"

Nate blinked. "Candle seems brighter than usual. Why's she doin' this to us, Bart? Makin' us into weird critters?"

Bart stared at him and shrugged. "I … I honestly have no idea, Nate. She keeps sayin' we're gonna make her a lotta money, but not how we're gonna do it."

Nate scratched at his ribs. The fur was already starting to spread from the grafted patches to his bare skin. The Stuff really did work fast. Bart wondered what it could do in the hands of someone who wanted to use it for good rather than evil.

Bart flopped onto his bed and lay on his back. He stared up at the mould patches on the ceiling. "Nate, I think I can help you find your mother."

Nate pushed himself up onto his elbows. "But Aunt Sissy is my mama!"

"No, she ain't!"

"Nate, I *seen* your mama, your real mama. She came here yes'day morning."

"You have? How'd ya know she was my real mama?"

"I overheard her talking to Aunt Sissy. We can leave here and go find her." Bart reached out to Nate, grabbed one of his hands and squeezed it. He knew if he could get through to Nate, give him the confidence to leave, they could run away from here together.

But Nate gulped. "I … I dunno, Bart." He looked up at the window. Bart hadn't pulled the curtain yet, and the sky was black. "It's dark and scary out there. Here we've got a bed, and food to eat, and toys to play with."

Bart sighed. Nate was still a little child, one of Sissy's works-in-progress; although he'd been altered, he wasn't treated nearly as badly as Bart was. He wasn't made to slave away all day long, performing dirty and dangerous chores. "All right, Nate. Good night." Bart got up, closed the curtain, and extinguished the candle on the little nightstand between their beds.

He lay down and closed his eyes, but tonight the thoughts that churned constantly through his mind wouldn't let him sleep. They did that sometimes, and he knew he wouldn't get any rest until he did something to soothe them.

Sissy was wrong about him. The Stuff he'd been exposed to had affected him far more than just causing him to grow an extra finger … an additional digit, he was discovering, that was helping him complete his increasing workload.

But the changes lay inside him, and the strange thoughts and his overactive imagination were mere side effects. Bart was *a lot* smarter than he let on, and he was getting smarter all the time. He could speed-read books now. Volumes he'd struggled with initially, he could now absorb in minutes and understand every word. Sometimes, late at night when he couldn't sleep, he read whole dictionaries and encyclopaedias. He could close his eyes and remember with total recall. Sometimes his brain felt like it was throbbing from all the knowledge filling it.

But tonight he had a different job to do.

* * *

A few hours later, Nate started awake. His new fur was itching again as it continued to spread around his body, but that wasn't what had roused him.

He could hear strange rumbling noises in the distance. Even though it didn't rain much here in Mojo Town, located as it was at the edge of a desert, he'd heard thunder a few times in his life. He didn't like it, and reached out for Bart, but his hand—*paw?*—touched a cold, empty bed. Nate pulled the blanket over his head and huddled underneath.

He lifted a thumb to suck, and nearly cut his lip on a fingernail that was already lengthening into a claw.

* * *

For all the next day and several days after that, Sissy used Bart as child labour, pushing him to do all manner of chores from sunup to sundown. Bart realised that she'd given up on him becoming anything more than a six-fingered boy. He would never be one of her freaks. He performed all the jobs as quickly and efficiently as he could—anything to avoid her chastisement, and maybe earn a nod or two of approval.

Anything to lull her into a false sense of security that he was the good, dull slave-boy she expected and wanted.

* * *

One evening after dinner, after Bart had completed his last chore, he led Nate up a rickety spiral staircase that led to the old house's attic. Nate followed behind on all fours. These days he did that occasionally, finding he was able to move just as easily in that manner. As Bart turned to check on him, he could see Nate's yellow eyes glowing in the half-light.

Bart figured he could get a few minutes of privacy, since Sissy and Zak never came up here. Sissy was too fat to fit up the narrow staircase, and Zak's dodgy legs were too unpredictable.

"Can you see right now?" Bart asked.

"Yeth," said Nate, lisping now because his upper lip was dividing into two, like a cat's. "But a lot paler."

"So you're not scared of the dark anymore?"

"No, cause it'th not really dark anymore."

At least that's positive news, Bart thought.

"Only thcared of the thunder," Nate continued.

"What thunder?"

"It thundered the other night. I heard it. When you were gone."

"But I didn't..." Bart tailed off. "Oh."

"Tho where'd you go?"

"Commode."

"You were gone a while."

"I was in there reading."

"Oh." Since reading was something Bart really liked doing, Nate couldn't question that. "Tho where we goin' now?"

Bart took him up into the attic, which stretched the entire width of the house. It still contained long-forgotten belongings of the house's previous inhabitants, piled up under the eaves and against the supports. Like the library downstairs, the rafters were shrouded with cobwebs and birds' nests. A cool wind blew in through cracks in the walls and roof tiles.

Bart expected Nate to be spooked, but he simply looked around in interest. He spotted movement out of the corner of one eye as a disturbed fowl fluttered from a nearby perch to one further away from the intruders. He spun around and raced after it. The piece of cat skin Sissy had left hanging at the base of his spine was starting to form into a proper tail, and flicked into the air as he moved.

"*Nate!*" Bart hissed.

Nate skidded to a stop, his claws clicking on the boards. "Thorry." Sheepishly he returned to Bart's side.

Bart reached into the man's dressing gown he wore as a coat and pulled out a jar he'd had tucked inside. The jar radiated a strange iridescent light. "Glow-worms," he explained as he handed it over.

Nate marvelled at the jar. "Where'd you git 'em?"

"Found 'em in the yard. Sissy had me muckin' out the pig pen today, and I spotted 'em just as the sun was setting, when I was dumping the last of the rubbish up the back."

The light from the glow-worms was soft and gentle, and gave their skin and immediate surroundings a yellow tinge.

"Pretty," Nate marvelled.

"I got somethin' else." Bart opened an old steamer trunk, reached in, and took out the newspaper he'd taken from Ma and Pa's conservatory. He passed it to Nate.

Nate put the glow-worms down on the floor and took the paper. He stared at it in confusion, twisting it this way and that. "But wot's it all about? I don't unnerstand it. I can't read like you. I tried an' tried, but it's thtill all thwiggles to me. I dunno how to make 'em into words."

Bart sighed. "If Aunt Sissy would just leave me alone for a bit, I could teach you." He pointed to a picture on the front page. "That's a SandSub." It depicted a long, sleek craft painted a sandy colour, about a quarter a mile long, with little portholes along its sides. It was designed to cruise through the desert sand dunes at a leisurely speed. It had a large, sharply-pointed wedge at the front, designed to break and push large rocks out of the way. The wedge was made of heavy mesh that let the fine sand particles pass underneath, where propellers funnelled them the length of the craft and spat them out the back. Thus the machine had the momentum it needed to move forward.

It was called the *SS Desert Devil*. The "SS" stood for "SandSub".

Quizzically, Nate studied the photo. "Wot's it for?"

"Cruisin' through the desert, of course. The desert stretches for hundreds of miles, an' people 'ave bin lookin' for a way to cross it for years. They tried trains an' trackless trains, but the sand kept gettin' into their engines and seizin' them dead. So the SandSub was invented. But till now they've only been small runabout ones that can slip through the dunes and zip between the rocks. Big enough for a couple of people at the most, an' not many supplies. The mechanologists didn't think a big sub was possible 'cause it wouldn't be able to pass through the rocky outcroppings. But the dunes are vast and the desert rocks are soft an' porous, and easily broken by this thing." Bart tapped the steel wedge at the front of the craft. "So they came up with this really big SandSub, the first of its kind."

Nate whistled. "It ith pretty big," he agreed. "So why you showin' me this?"

"It's gonna leave on its maiden voyage from Bhigge Smoche and we're gonna be on it."

Nate gaped at Bart in shock.

"It's so huge that no one will realise we're stowaways. If we just act normal, people'll think we're passengers. An' there'll be *plenty* of places to hide."

"Tho *that's* why you keep athkin' me to leave with you!" Nate exclaimed. Once again, he spotted something out of the corner of his eye.

This time he spun around to see a thin dark shape slide down from the ceiling. Anna, the Python Girl, had been curled around one of the rafters.

Bart whipped the paper behind his back, but it was too late. She'd obviously overheard everything. "What you doin' up here?" he demanded.

"Chasin' rats and birds." She licked her lips with her forked tongue. "Plenny o' them up here. Aunt Sissy's food just ain't enough for me anymore."

"A likely story. You follered us up here, din'tcha?"

"Maybe I did, maybe I didn't." She dropped to the dusty floorboards with a soft plop and rose up to face Bart. "I wanna come with you on the SandSub."

Bart and Nate exchanged worried glances. Bart really didn't want to take Anna along, but she knew too much and would definitely snitch on them.

Anna had a small purse slung across her sinuous body. With one tiny hand she took out the red lipstick Sissy had given her and painted her lips. She smiled at them. "I can keep a secret." She flickered her forked tongue again.

Bart turned back to Nate. "So, Nate—you wanna do this or not?"

Nate gulped. Truthfully, he was scared. But the strange changes he was undergoing were actually giving him more confidence. Not only was he no longer scared of the dark, but his reflexes were more acute. He could run faster and leap higher. He was actually starting to enjoy being a strange cat-human hybrid.

But he had no reason to stay, other than the creature comforts he enjoyed. Creature comforts that weren't being shared with Bart, whom Sissy worked like a slave.

He had to go. For his best friend's sake.

"All right," he said.

"We'll go tomorra night," said Bart. "Pack only what you can carry."

Anna nodded and smiled again.

The children crept back downstairs and separated in the corridor outside their rooms. Anna slithered off down the dark, quiet passage and disappeared. Bart wondered how she'd managed to escape from the dorm, as it was kept locked. But then again, she was a snake. She could probably squeeze through very tiny gaps now. Maybe she'd even escaped out of the little open window above the door.

He led Nate into their tiny room and closed the door behind them. "Pack yer stuff," he told Nate in a low voice as he pulled a battered old rucksack from under his bed and started stuffing his clothes into it. "We're leaving right now."

"But you thaid—"

Bart lifted a bony finger to his lips.

"But what about Anna? You promithed her."

"Yar, I knows it, but I think yer right. She really can't be trusted. She'll be goin' to sleep now. Best we leave her be. She'll be all right here—she has all the other kids wrapped around her little ... tail."

"Yar, all right." Nate experienced a flood of relief. He *really* didn't like Anna, and now that he was developing a cat's feelings, he found himself wanting to grab her in his jaws and shake her until her spine snapped. He hoped he wouldn't become too catlike. He packed his own meagre belongings, making sure he had sufficient clothes to cover his furry body.

Bart nudged the door open and looked right and left. He was fortunate Sissy didn't bother locking him and Nate in at night as well. Bart supposed this was because sometimes she kept him doing chores until well into the night.

Hefting their rucksacks, they snuck out and tiptoed past the big dorm. Bart led the way down the stairs, keeping close to the wall to avoid any creaks or groans from the old wood. He took Nate out through the back door and didn't close it behind him. He led Nate through the overgrown yard and through the rusty gate leading to the children's cemetery. He left that open as well.

"Where we goin'?" asked Nate in a whisper.

"The junkyard, but we hafta go the long way 'round. There's no gap in the wall, and it's too high to climb."

"Oh." Nate glanced over his shoulder. *I reckon I could jump on top of it now*, he thought, *but then how would I get Bart over?*

They followed the cemetery fence along to the back, and then slipped out through a hole. Here the ground was steep and treacherous, until they hooked up with the trail that led down into the crater. They crept along the orphanage's back fence and to the rear of the junkyard. Here part of a wall had collapsed, and because only the crater lay behind, nobody had bothered fixing it. Bart led Nate over the rubble and into the yard.

CHAPTER 13

The Mojo Town junkyard was surrounded by a high stone wall, with just a rusty gate at the front to allow people entry to dump their junk. It contained all the usual stuff found in dumps that no one wanted and couldn't burn or recycle, such as old mattresses, bed frames, mouldy pillows, rags, rusty saucepans, and such. But it also contained piles of decrepit machinery from all over town: broken stoves, parts from engines and mechanical horses, worn-out tools, and equipment from the power plant.

Through the stinking, teetering piles of rubbish, Bart led the way to a big derelict wagon lying upside down against one of the garbage heaps. Its wheels and axles had been removed. Huge fat rats, who'd probably been down into the crater and affected by the Stuff, darted away as the children approached. Nate wanted to chase after them, but managed to resist the urge.

Bart slipped into the gap that had been created by the wagon's tilt.

Nate followed, his cat-eyes widening at the sight of all the glow-worms attached to the walls and ceiling.

"Sorry," said Bart. "*This* is where I found 'em."

"Ya didn't actually lie," said Nate. "You thaid you found 'em in the yard. You never thaid *which* yard!" He giggled. It sounded like a meow.

Bart laughed too, and stepped over to something in the centre of the wagon; something hidden beneath an old canvas tarp.

"What ith that?" Nate asked.

Bart pulled back the sheet to reveal his secret project. Nate's eyes nearly came out on stalks. Using bits and pieces scavenged from around the junkyard, Bart had built a small, souped-up road-hugging buggy. It had eight wheels for stability—four from the wagon and four from a carriage. They'd been reinforced with steel rims. At the front he'd installed an engine from a mechanical carriage, but it didn't have a boiler or chimney. Where they should have been was a round metal canister with a funnel at the front. Various pipes and hoses led from it, directly into the workings of the engine. A tap at the base of the canister controlled the flow—of what, Nate had no idea. The control reins had been attached to either side of a makeshift T-shaped steering column. Beside it was some sort of control board with various buttons attached. Green cables trailed from them to the engine. A compass was also attached.

At the back of the dangerous-looking contraption Bart had bolted a bench seat wide enough for three small people, and had installed a framework over it so it could be covered with canvas whenever the weather deteriorated. He tossed his bag onto the seat and gestured for Nate to do the same.

"Wh-what ith it?" Nate gasped.

"It's like a small low stagecoach. I call it a speed-buggy."

"Where did it come from?"

"I built it," Bart answered, unable to keep the pride from his voice.

Nate couldn't believe his senses. "How'n heck did you do that?"

"To be honest, I dunno. Somehow I just knew what to do. I guess there must've bin enough information in all the books I read for me to be able to piece all the bits together." Bart tapped his forehead.

Nate planted his hands on his hips. "Why dint'cha tell me?" His lisp was receding as he adapted to his feline form.

"It was a secret, and the more people who knew about it, the more who'd find out."

Nate nodded. "Awright. So what's it do?"

"It's what's gonna take us to Bhigge Smoche, to where the *SS Desert Devil*'s leaving. What—didja think we were gonna walk all the way?" Bart unscrewed a lid from the funnel. "Luckily I got most of it built before Sissy added more chores for me."

"However didja find the time ta make this? It musta taken ya months!"

"It did take me months. But these days I don't sleep as much as I used to. So since Aunt Sissy upped my workload, I bin sneakin' out late at night while everyone's asleep. Then Sissy got me goin' down the crater by meself to gather the Stuff ... an' that turned into a real opportunity." Bart bent down, picking up something he'd kept under the machine, in between its wheels.

It was a full glass canister of the Stuff, glowing a brilliant green in the light of the glow-worms.

* * *

Bart explained to Nate about what had happened one day, when he'd gone down into the crater alone to gather the Stuff. Unlike Sissy, he'd made sure to wear gloves and galoshes while collecting it. He didn't want to be cutting off weird growths in the future. But even though he was careful, his compass still slipped out of his shirt pocket and plopped into the Stuff. He'd found that compass in the dump, and it still worked perfectly. He didn't want to lose it. So, gritting his teeth, he dipped his gloved hand into the thick green mire. Icy cold seeped through the thick rubber, but he'd managed to fish the thing out.

He'd brought water with him to drink, and poured some over the device to clean it, but it still felt weird and different, cold and heavier than before. Its needle quivered wildly, even when he held it still. Bart dried it with a rag and stuffed it back in his pocket. Then he returned with the Stuff, which he delivered to Sissy, who smiled and told him he'd been a good boy … for once.

Later that day he felt a stirring in his shirt pocket, then a sharp sting in his chest, like a wasp had crept inside and attacked him. He yelped and clapped a hand to his pocket. He yanked out the compass and discovered that thin green tendrils had sprouted from the small gaps and cracks in its surface. They were writhing wildly. One had blood on its tip, which was slowly sinking into its smooth surface as he watched. Obviously this one had tried to burrow into his body. He shuddered, realising that he'd only just gotten the compass out in time.

He had to find somewhere to hide it, and the best place he could think of was the junkyard. He placed the compass on top of the buggy's control board.

The next night, he returned to tinker some more with the machine and found that green tendrils had extended from the compass and grown around the cables from the control board, turning them green, and extending down into the buggy's engine. Fearing all his good work would be lost, Bart struggled to prise the device off. Although the Stuff stretched like rubber, it was far too thick and strong for him to break, and it appeared to have infiltrated the engine's entire workings. It was too deeply entrenched, and appeared to have become one with the buggy. He'd never be able to flush it out.

Bart stepped back and scratched his head, wondering what on Earth to do. But then he remembered how the Stuff had brought that bird back from the dead. Could it also animate mechanical devices? If so, then that just might be the very thing he needed to complete his project.

"That rumbling you heard in the middle of the night wasn't thunder," Bart told Nate. "It was me test-driving the speed-buggy. I took it up and down Boneyard Way three times. It ran perfectly. An' the compass still works, too."

* * *

Bart continued his story. The next time Sissy sent him down into the crater to gather the Stuff, he made two trips instead of one, hiding his first load under the buggy.

It was hard work clambering up and down the crater's steep sides, and he skinned his knees more times than he cared to count, but more than worth it to build up a secret stash of the Stuff inside his junkyard hideout.

* * *

Bart handed Nate the canister and then ducked down again. He brought out two more full containers, green and glowing in the glow-worms' light.

"So much!" Nate gasped.

Bart started to pull the glow-worms down from the ceiling and pop them into small glass jars. "We're gonna need a lot of these for the trip." He placed two of the jars on the ground and up-ended one of the Stuff canisters, pouring some of the green goo into each. Suddenly the glow-worms flared into brilliant white life. Nate hissed—just like a cat—and scuttled off a few steps.

"We're gonna need light if we wanna travel at night," Bart explained as he hooked the glow-worm jars onto the front of the buggy, one on each side of the engine. "The Stuff makes 'em glow brighter, but they'll only last a few hours." He shoved the remaining jars of worms into his pack. "Spares for later. You ready?"

"Um…" Suddenly Nate detected a sound behind him, and whirled around to see Anna slithering under the edge of the overturned wagon.

"I'm ready to go too," she declared in her soft, sweet voice. She was carrying her small purse slung over one shoulder, and a larger bag over the other. She was even wearing a bonnet festooned with flowers, tied neatly around her neck. Her long braids hung down around her slender body. "I figured you musta made a mistake when you said you's goin' tomorrow night instead o' tonight."

Bart managed to wipe the shock from his face, and broke into a wide false smile: "Anna! I was just about to run back and get you. I needed some time to prepare the machine."

Anna smiled and flickered her forked tongue: "I saved you the trouble." She slithered up to the buggy and slid inside onto the seat, where she curled herself up just like the snake she was.

Bart and Nate reached down to pick up the canisters on the ground beside the engine. Nate glanced over his shoulder at Anna sitting primly in the buggy. She was applying her lipstick again. "She's always sneakin' up on us. I hate how she does that," he whispered into Bart's ear.

"Me too," Bart whispered back. "But we gotta take her with us now, or she'll tattle on us!"

Bart poured his canister of Stuff into the funnel on top of the container above the engine, and bade Nate to do the same. The last one he placed on the floor of the cab. "Can you hold this for us, Anna?" he asked. "Don't want it to smash."

Anna smiled and dropped her tail down to curl around it.

Bart got Nate to lift the side of the wagon while he pushed the speed-buggy out into the junkyard. Then both boys manoeuvred it through the front of the junkyard. They tried to be as quiet as they could, lest they wake Sissy and Zak. The lads managed to shove the buggy out through the gates and onto Boneyard Way. Bart spun the tap at the bottom of the canister to start the flow of Stuff into the engine. Then the boys scrambled aboard the contraption, and it started to roll down the hill.

The buggy coughed into life and ignited with a throaty roar.

"It works, it really works!" Nate clapped his paws, bouncing up and down on his seat in excitement. "I don't believe it! We're ridin' up high like rich toffs!"

Bart grinned. "Yar, that we are!" He glanced at Anna against the other side, but she looked completely cool and complacent, like she did this sort of thing all the time. Her blonde braids bounced in the cool night air. Suddenly realising that Bart was looking at her, she turned and smiled sweetly at him, flicking her tongue at him. Then she put her head down on her coils and closed her eyes. Her tail remained coiled around the container on the floor, looped around itself so it wouldn't come untied.

They rumbled down from the hill and along the main drag through the middle of Mojo Town. At this time of night the settlement was dark and quiet, but the strange noise of the engine brought a few insomniacs out onto their front porches to stare in disbelief as the bizarre contraption passed. They'd never seen anything like it, and had no idea where it had come from. Most dismissed it as a product of their overactive, sleep-deprived minds.

Bart twisted the steering column. The buggy wasn't particularly manoeuvrable, but he managed to turn into the Mule Train Depot and start following the dusty road used by the trackless train.

Nate scratched at one of his arms. His new fur was itching again. He pulled his dressing gown close and lifted its hood, covering his distinctive ears. He was outside the orphanage now—he couldn't afford to let anyone see his cat-features. "So how do yer know where to go?"

Bart tapped the compass on the control-board. "This will point us in the right direction. We just gotta head east, and look!" He pointed at the road ahead. In the eerie light of the enhanced glow-worms, the trackless train's path could be clearly seen, the ruts in the dust where nothing grew.

He pulled the T-shaped steering column towards him, and the speed-buggy started to accelerate from its stately pace to a faster velocity. Its rumble graduated to a throaty roar. Since the trackless train's path was smooth, this didn't result in too much uncomfortable bouncing, and Bart was able to increase speed still further, until he was going faster than the train. *A lot* faster.

Nate whistled. "We're really movin' now."

"Oh, yar. At this rate we'll be in Bhigge Smoche by dawn."

"Woo-ee, this is fun! I have *nevah* moved this fast before in my life! Why do we even *need* to go on the SandSub? We could ride around the countryside in this!"

"It is nice, but it'll only take us so far. When the Stuff runs out, we'll just stop." Bart gestured off to one side, and Nate noticed a light mist issuing from the engine as the used Stuff evaporated into the atmosphere. "I have no idea if there's any more Stuff anywhere else in the West. P'raps the only source of it is in our crater. But there should be enough of it to get us to Bhigge Smoche, to where the SandSub is."

"Won't Bhigge Smoche be far enough fer us? I heard that the city is huge and people git lost in it all the time."

"Mebbe so, but I want us to git as far away as possible. The SandSub will cross the Mighty Desert and takes us all the way to Tutherside. That's like the other end of the West. Sissy an' Zak will never be able to foller us all the way there."

"What if they catch us before we can git on the sub?"

Bart reached out and patted Nate's shoulder. "Don't worry. I've set up a diversion that'll keep 'em busy for quite a while."

"What?"

"Just before dinner I went into the cemetery and shoved pipes into the graves of some of Sissy's more recent failures. She gets Zak to bury 'em after they die, but he's too lazy to dig six feet down. The graves are no more'n a couple feet deep at the most. I poured some Stuff down there, an' by my reckoning those dead kids should be wakin' right about now."

Nate gaped at Bart in horror. "Wh-what?" he gasped.

"Just like that dead bird."

Nate couldn't believe his senses. How could his friend *do* something so horrible? "But—but they was our brothers 'n' sisters!" he finally managed to gasp.

"Yes," Bart said softly. "They *was*. But they ain't no more. Their souls are gone, to heaven, or the afterlife, or wherever we go after we die. What's left behind is just *materials*."

* * *

Back at the cemetery, on the hill beneath the dead oak tree, bony hands and various other mutated appendages started to thrust up out of the ground. Zombie children began to crawl from the dirt. Most were in advanced states of decay, some desiccated, others still with strips of flesh falling from their bones, but the Stuff had formed into glowing green strands around their bodies, serving to hold them together and grant them a strange sort of un-life. These were the children who'd been unable to handle Sissy's bizarre experiments; either they were too weak, or more likely the changes had been just too extreme for their young bodies to handle.

A scorpion boy scuttled along on six arms, holding two more out in front of them. These were festooned with sharp claws instead of hands. A girl, sort of a predecessor to Anna, writhed along on a nest of serpents sprouting from her hips. Another looked relatively normal, save for the dozen eyes growing from his forehead on stalks. A fourth child had a row of arms growing from his back and lumbered along on four short, thick legs.

In total, eight mutant zombie children had risen from their shallow graves, and they roamed around the cemetery until the boy with all the eyes discovered the open gate leading to the orphanage. The gate that Bart had oh-so-conveniently left open just for them.

The Stuff activated whatever it could find in the children's brains that was still intact. As small portions of their memories fired up, they realised their surroundings were familiar. They remembered that most of them had died because of Sissy's unholy experiments upon their innocent bodies. But most importantly, the ground was cold and lonely, while the interior of the orphanage was warm and dry, with hot food waiting for them inside, to satisfy the endless hunger boiling in their bellies.

They clambered up onto the back veranda and fumbled around, looking for a way in. Eventually they found the back door, which Bart had also left ajar. They shuffled inside and rummaged through the kitchen, yanking open cupboards and upending drawers. They found the big pots where Sissy boiled up her vile porridge and stew. Both still had some sludge in the bottom, which would undoubtedly be used for future meals. But the children didn't care, and upended both on the floor so they could lap up the residue.

Eventually their racket woke the children on the level directly above, and they started to cry. Their cries woke Sissy, and she scrambled ponderously out of bed, yanked on her dressing gown, and roused Zak from his deep sleep. Her brother snorted awake with a start.

They grabbed whatever weapons they could find and stumbled downstairs, where the zombie children were completely trashing the kitchen in their insatiable search for more food. They'd already emptied containers of flour and oats, ripped open bags of dried fruit, and consumed strips of preserved meat Sissy had been saving for leaner months.

The infuriated siblings laid into the creatures with their weapons. Sissy had a fire poker, and Zak used his trusty cane.

Upstairs, the hefty mutant child Rex managed to get the dorm room door open simply by running into it at high speed. He led a charge downstairs into the kitchen, joining in the fight against the zombie horde. They charged in tooth and claw to defend their home. Unfortunately, despite their various new abilities, they didn't know how to fight, and some of the children, such as the ferocious Rex and Spider Boy, were badly mauled in the process.

Eventually Sissy, Zak, and her mutant children managed to drive the zombies from the kitchen and back out into the yard, but significant damage was done in the process. The big pots were destroyed, the stove smashed, the walls and floor torn up, the doors ripped from their frames.

"Bart, *Bart!*" Sissy yelled, but he didn't answer.

Out in the yard, Zak managed to stave in the last of the zombies' heads, leaving them as limp heaps of flesh on the ground. The Stuff infecting their bodies continued to glow and made them quiver, but since they were now so badly damaged, they could no longer rise. The mutant children backed off to catch their breath and take stock.

Sissy counted the kids who'd come down to help, and then hurried upstairs to check on the ones who'd stayed and cowered in their rooms. She expected to find Anna there, but she was nowhere to be seen. She yanked open the door to Bart and Nate's room, and found their beds empty as well.

Sissy couldn't remember seeing Bart, Nate, and Anna come down to help, but everything had been so chaotic in the kitchen, with flour and grain flying everywhere, obscuring visibility, and everyone fighting tooth and nail. Perhaps those ravenous undead mutants had eaten the three missing children.

"Zak, you start cleanin' this mess while I get these kids fixed up an' back inta bed," she ordered her brother.

Zak rolled his eyes; usually Bart did this sort of thing. But Sissy's expression was so thunderous that he simply sighed loudly and reached for a broom.

Sissy led the kids back upstairs into their dorm, fetched some iodine and bandages from the bathroom, and set to work tending to their wounds. Then she tucked them into their beds, brought them tea, and waited until they'd settled down. Exhaustion soon took over, and they quickly fell asleep.

Sissy heaved her huge bulk up and lumbered back downstairs, where Zak was grumbling and muttering as he was shovelling the huge pile of wasted food he'd swept into a corner onto a wheelbarrow for the pigs. "Blasted things are gonna eat better'n us," he complained. "I'll fix the stove and doors tomorra," he told Sissy.

"That's fine, but you'd better go'n bury the dead kids now, before they git up again. They's infected with active Stuff, in case ya didn't notice. It might regenerate 'em."

"How'n hell did active Stuff git into their graves?"

"How'n hell would *I* know, ya dumb bastard?" Sissy tossed her hands into the air. "Jus' make sure you bury 'em good an' deep this time, so they cain't claw their way out again!"

Zak swore under his breath as he stomped out into the yard, resigning himself to the grim fact that he wouldn't get any sleep tonight and his thumping headache wouldn't improve. But as he was dragging the corpses back into the graveyard, to the disturbed graves, he noticed a couple of intact ones with strange funnels thrust into them. Green Stuff glistened around the rims.

CHAPTER 14

Bart thought about stopping so they could camp for the night, but he wasn't tired, and besides, Anna was already sleeping peacefully in a pile of coils, and Nate was leaning against him with his eyes closed, obviously exhausted. So he continued on into the night, along the trackless train's path through the scrubby hills, until a few hours later, when the glow-worms inside his jar-lights started to flicker and die. He slowed to a stop, gently lifted Nate from him, and fished out the remaining jars he'd packed. He lifted the container of Stuff from Anna's coils and poured some into the jars of worms, illuminating two new sets.

He climbed down and walked around to the front of the machine, where he unhooked the old jars. He lifted one up to examine it just as the last worm sputtered and died. It sank to the bottom of the container, joining its dead fellows. The Stuff had desiccated the tiny creatures into flat, nearly-weightless skins. *Interesting*, Bart thought.

He hooked up the new jars and left the old ones beside the road.

Then he poured the last of the Stuff into the engine, tossed the empty container onto the ground beside the jars, and returned to his seat. As he climbed back in, Nate mumbled something and shifted position, curling up in a ball like a cat. Beside him, Anna never stirred.

Slowly Bart accelerated away, and their journey resumed.

Later, as the sun started to peep over the horizon, Bart noticed a smoky cloud directly ahead. *What is that?* he wondered. *It's directly in our path!* But as he approached, shapes began to form in the gloom: tall buildings, shrouded in smoke.

He was looking at the city of Bhigge Smoche. He couldn't believe his senses. His insane plan had worked, and his bizarre contraption had actually carried them all the way. They'd made it!

Nate lifted his head and blinked. Low-roofed bungalows began to pass on either side, lying well back from the road on carefully-cultivated plots of land. Long shadows from lush green trees began to fall across the road.

"We're here?" gasped Nate.

"Yes." Bart responded. "Now we've just gotta work out where to go."

The dirt road gave way to cobblestone streets, and the bungalows transformed into taller houses with smaller yards, then townhouses joined together in neat rows. By this stage Anna had woken up too, and was peering out around the canvas canopy with interest. Other vehicles had started to appear on the early morning streets: mechanical horses, carts, and carriages, controlled by tired-looking deliverymen. Bart slowed down to a sedater pace to avoid running into them. A few heads turned to look at his strange contraption, and eyes widened as people realised they'd never seen such a weird-looking vehicle.

All three kids, used to clean country air marred only by the occasional tinge of smoke from the local power plant or foundry, started to cough from the stench coming from all the manufactories to the east.

Bart slowed the speed-buggy to a crawl. He could tell it was starting to run out of power. "We're gonna hafta ditch this conveyance soon." He twisted the T-shaped steering column, turning into a side street that looked relatively deserted. "We don't have no more Stuff to keep runnin' it." He rumbled down the street, which was lined with tall wooden fences. Behind them lay the long narrow yards belonging to the townhouses. The double gates of one were propped open, revealing a cluttered space filled with old pieces of machinery, some rusting out in the open, others hidden beneath awnings and tarps. "Perfect!" Bart cried, and drove into the yard.

And just in time, for the engine started to cough and splutter. Bart jumped down, closely followed by Nate. They pushed the vehicle up as far as it would go, and then collected their bags. Anna slithered down, landing on the dusty ground with a plop.

Bart turned the taps, cutting off the last of the flow, and the engine died. An early morning silence fell, punctuated by the distant rattle of wooden and steel wheels on cobbles. Bart stared at the machine.

"What's up?" asked Nate. "Ain't we gonna continue on foot now?"

Bart didn't answer. He continued to stare at the speed-buggy as though the younger boy hadn't spoken. Nate opened his mouth to ask him again, but then Bart patted the side of the engine and said, "You got us here in one piece, but now we gotta leave you. I hope someone finds you and kin figger out howta make you into somethin' better."

Nate closed his mouth. Bart turned to face him.

"Let's go before someone sees us."

Nate made sure the hood of his dressing gown was pulled up and shadowing his face. The gown was pretty long and covered him to his ankles, hiding his increasingly mobile tail. But Anna, as a snake-girl, would be harder to conceal.

Bart spotted something partially hidden under one of the tarps, and raced over to it. He pulled out a dilapidated but still functional perambulator. He gestured excitedly. "In here, Anna!"

Anna turned her nose up at it. "In there? You can't be serious! It's filthy!"

"We can't 'ave you slitherin' along beside us like our pet snake! People'll stare—an' more importantly, *remember*."

She rolled her eyes at him. "Oh, awright, dang it!"

Bart pushed the pram on its side, brushed the dust and dirt out of it, and Anna slithered in and curled up. He pulled some clothes from his bag, tucking them around her like blankets. In her cute little bonnet, she looked like an adorable toddler, until Nate snickered at her and she hissed at him.

"Not funny!" she spat.

Nate covered his mouth. Bart glared at him. "Come on—we still gotta find where the SandSub's gonna leave from. I got no idea, so we gotta ask someone. We can't afford to be too suspicious-lookin'."

"Yes, Bart," said Nate and Anna together.

Bart piled their rucksacks under the pram and grabbed its handle. He took one last look at his machine, and then gazed around the yard at all the other wonderful devices. He wished he could stay here and examine the machines more closely. But they had a job to do, a mission to Tutherside to complete.

He trundled the old pram from the yard, and Nate followed.

* * *

A few hours later, the back door of the townhouse flew open with a crash and one very hung-over Sidney Chrome staggered out into the yard, blinking repeatedly in the late morning sunlight. He'd just woken up from a big night of booze and partying with his clockworker Betty, whom he'd recently upgraded and re-upholstered. She'd performed satisfactorily—*more* than satisfactorily, in fact. Sid was badly bruised in places and needed to loosen a few rubber sphincters before he could continue with any more frolic.

But right now, the mad inventor thought he was still hallucinating from all the absinthe he'd drunk.

Parked in the middle of his yard was a bizarre contraption that looked like a mechanical carriage that someone had built themselves from whatever they'd found lying around. Sid had never seen anything like it, and he wandered around it several times to make sure it was actually real. He removed the brainwaver he wore nearly every waking moment, just in case it had started malfunctioning on him.

The weird buggy remained.

Sid scratched his head in confusion.

* * *

Meanwhile, back at the orphanage, Zak spent all day digging deeper graves for the dead children, rolling their bodies in and burying them. He had to stop every time someone entered the cemetery, which was unusual. It was rare for anybody to venture to the cemetery, but for some unknown reason there was a steady flow of visitors today. Not a huge number, but still irritating enough to someone who just wanted to get the damn job finished. He also had to pause to repeatedly whack the dead bodies with his shovel, because despite their staved-in heads, they just kept *twitching*. The Stuff was still active, and continued trying to do its work. Sissy came out to give him food and drink to keep him going, but by the end of the day he was dirty, sweaty, and extremely pissed off.

The sun was setting by the time Zak was patting down the last of the graves with his shovel. He straightened up with a curse and a crick in his back, and turned his head to look down on the town in the valley below. Gaslights and candles were winking on in the poorer sections, and electric lamps in the richer ones. But he also spotted something else, something that served to lift his ragged spirits.

Strange lights in the sky moved slowly towards the centre of town. They illuminated the smooth curve of a huge, rounded object—the giant gas-filled belly of the Watkins Desertboat Zeppelin!

Zak couldn't believe his senses. He felt like it hadn't visited Mojo Town in a decade, but in reality it showed up every year or so. He tossed down his shovel and staggered inside the house as quickly as his unsteady legs would take him. He washed himself at the well outside, and crept into the house as quietly as he could.

Sissy was still in the dining room, feeding the children. The chore was taking her longer than normal because her usual assistant Bart wasn't around to help. Zak tiptoed past the dining room door, and she didn't see him. He hurried upstairs, changed his clothes, then snuck into Sissy's room and marched straight over to her tallboy.

Inside the drawer, hidden amongst her enormous under-things, Zak found the large roll of cash she thought she'd hidden from him. Next to the money was a water-globe. He had forgotten about it. He remembered giving it to Sissy long ago. *She'd kept it all this time?* he mused.

Zak picked up the water-globe and turned it around. The label on the front was tarnished, but he could still make out the scroll lettering which read "Rosewell".

Inside the glass dome primly sat a pretty fairytale house. He gave the globe a single shake and tiny white flakes rose, then gently fell upon the house.

What a sentimental old fool, Zak thought to himself.

Zak replaced the water-globe in the drawer and snatched up the wad of cash. Grabbing his cane and donning his best hat, he stole from the house and headed out to the barn.

He rolled out a battered mechanical mule with mis-matched wheels and twine wrapped around its body, and fired up the boiler. While waiting for it to heat up, he pushed the machine out through the front gates of the orphanage, onto Boneyard Way. When the engine finally came to life with a throaty roar, it was enough to bring Sissy running from the house.

She thundered out onto the front veranda. "Zak, *Zak*! Where'n hell d'yer think yer going?! *Zachariah Spindler, you come back here right now!*"

Seated astride the ancient mechanical mule with his knees sticking out like wings, Zak rolled down toward town with an excited grin on his face. It was time for some *fun*!

Sissy blinked and spotted the distant lamps of the Watkins Desertboat Zeppelin, shining down on the big square at the centre of town. Ropes had been made fast around the spire at the top of the town hall, and gangways extended from the roof to the craft so people could board.

Sissy bared her fang-like teeth in a furious snarl. "*Damn* that miserable old coot, leavin' me here alone to tend to the chillen while he goes off and whoops it up!" An awful suspicion formed, and she raced back inside.

Opening her tallboy drawer, she found her giant knickers crumpled aside and her water-globe disturbed. She reached inside, hoping against hope, but he had taken all their savings. "Ooooh, I'm gonna bloody well *kill you*!"

* * *

The Watkins Desertboat Zeppelin had been securely tethered to the town hall spire. The big fan at its rear spun slowly, just enough to keep it stable in the cool evening breeze. Smoke puffed leisurely from its twin funnels. Unable to contain his excitement, Zak joined the crowds of Mojo Town's finest in their Sunday best. Clockworker attendants in top hats and tails stood on either side of the entrance, taking the $10 entrance fee. A few tried to negotiate the fee, but the impassive clockworkers were immune to haggling and wouldn't accept anything less.

Zak used $250 of Sissy's money to buy his way into a high-stakes poker game. He was sure he could win it back and more; the man running it didn't look much more than nineteen, and resembled a big fop with his fancy silkshot waistcoat and long curly moustache.

"Awright, let's 'ave a round of drinks here for my new friends!" the poker player called to one of the clockworker barmaids. She wore a wig of thick blonde curls, a corset, and a pair of those new fandangled pantaloons so she could move around easier.

"Yes, Mr McCade," said the clockworker, and directed her attention to the players. "What would you gentlemen like?"

Two grizzled old-timers ordered Cactus Wine and Viper Venom, a woman in a fur coat ordered some Tarantula Hair, and McCade asked for a shot of Red Eye.

"And you, sir?" the clockworker asked Zak.

"Um … beer?"

"Beer? What is this? Breakfast time?" shouted McCade. "Bring this man some Saddle Sore!" The clockworker scurried off. McCade gave a wicked grin. "Only the best for my poker team!"

When the drinks arrived, everyone chugged theirs down except for Zak, who sipped tentatively at his. He was used to his homebrewed elderberry wine, which wasn't much more alcoholic than beer. This rot-gut could strip the varnish from the chairs.

Tugging on one side of his moustache, McCade looked sideways at Zak. *Can't trust a man who don't drink straight up*, he thought. "What are you, mister? A man or a mouse? My ninety-year-old grandma can consume whiskey faster'n that! C'mon, drink up, drink up! Quickly now! We need ta git this party started!" He clapped his hands.

Zak took another sip. He still had half of his small glass left, and was already feeling extremely light-headed. He was considering ordering the obnoxious young whippersnapper not to rush him when he felt something poke him under the table, right in the belly.

Slowly he looked down to the sight of the barrel of a revolver, thrust into his guts.

"I said *drink up*," McCade declared pointedly.

Zak couldn't believe his senses, and looked around to see if the clockworkers had noticed. One in a fancy suit was standing only a few feet away, looking right at them. Then it turned and wandered off in response to a fat man furiously beckoning it over. It obviously didn't care one iota.

Zak tossed the drink back in one gulp and immediately started coughing and spluttering, his eyes watering. Everyone around him, including McCade, laughed uproariously.

Satisfied, McCade secreted his hold-out pistol with a smirk. Now he knew for sure what sort of poker player Zak would be. He might have been dressed like a gentleman in that nice hat and threads, but he was quite obviously new money. And more importantly, *easy* money.

"Awright, lady and gents, let's play poker!"

CHAPTER 15

Bart, Nate, and Anna learnt fairly quickly where the *SS Desert Devil* was leaving from, but it took them the better part of a day to navigate through Bhigge Smoche's crowded, labyrinthine streets to reach the big new depot on the south side of the city. The three country children had never seen so many people crammed into one place, smelled so many weird scents, or experienced so much noise. By the end of the day they were tired, hungry, and feeling extremely claustrophobic from all the tall, dark buildings towering over them, and the overhanging wires that were, in places, so thick they diminished the sun.

"I don't think it's far now," Bart told Nate and Anna. "But it's gettin' dark. We need ta find somewhere to sleep. I, fer one, am exhausted."

"How 'bout down there?" Nate pointed a claw down a gloomy side street. A large row of barrels provided a secluded hiding place.

"Looks as good as anywhere else." Bart pushed the pram containing Anna into the dark alley, and as soon as they were out of sight of the crowds on the main street, Anna slithered out.

"Where you goin'? You should stay put!" Bart chastised.

She flickered her tongue at him. "I bin cooped up in that silly baby thang all day! I'm off for a bit of a slither an' maybe find myself a fat mouse or rat to eat!"

In response to that, Nate's stomach growled. He couldn't believe how good a meal of rodent sounded. He looked mournfully at Bart. "Ken I go too?"

"What? No! Someone'll see you!"

Nate shrugged off his dressing gown and dropped onto all fours. "It's dark an' I'm a cat now. Cats are quiet. Please?"

Bart sighed. It would save him from trying to think of what to feed him. "Oh, awright. Just be careful, for pity's sake!"

Nate flicked his tail and was gone into the shadows just like ... well, a cat. Bart stared after him in disbelief. The boy really was becoming in tune with his new feline nature, just like Anna was in tune with hers.

Bart rubbed his stomach, wondering what to do about his own hunger. He wandered back up the lane to its mouth and looked up and down the main street. He noticed across the road a shabby, had-seen-grander-days tavern called the Buckhorn Palace Saloon, and beside it, something called the Sweet Sugar Shack. The big glass window was full of delicious-looking pastries.

He thought he might be able to scavenge something from either the back of the tavern or the bakery, but then he noticed a rather ominous-looking two-headed indian lurking in the alleyway between the saloon and bakery. Hoping the fellow hadn't spotted him, Bart quickly retreated back into the hiding space behind his barrels and hunkered down. He was far too tired to risk sneaking past that fellow now. Better to try in the morning, when he was rested and he had his friends with him. With a sigh he sat down in a doorway, curled his knees up to his chest, and rested his head on them. He might have been the brains of the group, but he was stuck here alone now, tired and hungry, while

Anna and Nate were off hunting dinner. They were far better equipped to survive than he was.

Bart closed his eyes and must have dropped off immediately, for the next thing he knew, he was being roughly shaken awake.

"You carn sleep here! This is my spot!" a loud voice slurred, breathing stale whiskey fumes all over him.

Bart lurched upright, facing a hairy drunk dressed in a filthy, ragged coat. He was carrying a bottle in one hand. He may have been unsteady on his feet, but he was quite large, towering over the boy. Bart didn't have a hope in hell of beating him in a fight. "Awright, awright—I'll be movin' along. Just lemme grab my—" He tried to reach for the pram, but the drunk caught it first.

"Ya in my spot, so this is mine too. Got some nice clothes in it."

Bart curled his hands into fists in a fury. He was heartily sick of being small and constantly bullied by big thugs who thought they could get away with it. "It most certainly is not!"

The drunk simply laughed at the tiny kid's bravado and shoved him before he could react, knocking him onto his backside on the cobblestones.

Then something plummeted from the sky and landed on the drunk, slamming him to the ground in front of Bart. Nate, his eyes glowing in the dark and his long white fangs gleaming, hissed in the drunk's face.

The drunk shrieked and started scrambling backwards along the ground, still screaming and gibbering.

"*Shaddap down there!*" someone roared from a window high above.

Nate gathered himself for a leap. Somehow the drunk managed to get his legs under him and sprint off. He struck a barrel in the process, sending it clattering down the alley. Nate retrieved it and brought it back so they could continue to have their hiding place. He sat down beside his friend. "Sorry 'bout that, Bart. Took me a while to find a rat, but it smelled funny and tasted horrible. Like it was full of poisons or somethin'." He stuck his tongue out in disgust.

Bart patted him on a shoulder. "It's fine, Nate. I think I found us a place that might have some food. We'll check it out tomorrow. Where's Anna?"

As though on cue, the snake girl came sliding around the barrels, her long tongue flickering. She was still wearing her pretty bonnet. She slithered up into the pram and curled herself into a ball.

"Did you find somethin' to eat?" asked Bart.

"A big, fat rat."

"I et one too. Did yours taste funny?" Nate asked her.

"Dunno. Swallered it whole." She lowered her head, disappearing from sight.

Bart went back to the stoop and sank down. Nate curled up beside him, falling asleep almost immediately. Bart closed his eyes, but after his scare it took him a lot longer to return to sleep. He ended up slumping forward across Nate's slumbering body, using his warm, furry form as a pillow.

Bart only stirred when Nate moved, padding off down the gloomy alley to find a gutter to relieve himself into. Bart jumped to his feet before he was completely awake, looking wildly around. Anna stuck her head from her pram, straightening her bonnet with her tiny hands, and gave him a look of disdain. Somewhat embarrassed, Bart straightened up and smoothed down his dressing-gown. Nate stalked up to him, swishing his long tail from side to side. He collected the robe he'd discarded the previous night and slipped it back on, covering his unique features.

"We got company." The cat boy gestured with a paw. Bart blinked, noticing, in the grim grey light of dawn, a humped shape at the end of their little side street. Remembering what had happened the night before, he approached cautiously. Nate stuck close, in case his teeth and claws were required.

Bart soon found himself standing over a dirty figure slumped in the gutter. It was dressed in rags and stank abominably, like it had soiled itself numerous times. Bart wondered if someone had chosen their street as a place to die in during the night. Cautiously he prodded the figure, and suddenly the creature gave a loud snort and rolled over, expelling a variety of noxious gases from various orifices. It flopped into the drain, arms spread wide, staring unseeingly at the slowly-brightening sky. Little bubbles of drool popped at the corners of its mouth. Bart backed away in horror.

"What in tarnation?" gasped Nate. "Is he the drunk who bothered ya last night?"

Bart shuddered. "Nevah seen no drunk look like that, Nate! He looks like he's starin' into the eyes of hell itself."

Carefully, the three children avoided the strange, semi-conscious derelict. But he never moved or gave any sign that he'd heard them. They managed to get their pram to the mouth of their street without being noticed. Across lay the tavern and bakery Bart had spotted the night before. At the sight of all those delicious pastries in the window, all three began salivating in hunger, even those who'd managed to get a meal of rat the night before.

But then there was that semi-naked two-headed indian, covered in tattoos and dressed in nothing but a greasy loincloth, lurking in the exact same spot he'd been in the night before, almost as though he had never left. Bart had been hoping he might have gone off to have a rest, but he looked as alert as ever.

As the kids watched, a shabby-looking lowlife, dressed in a tunic pocked with holes, approached the indian. He looked around, making sure no one was watching too closely, and stuck out a filthy hand. The indian's two heads leered, and he held out one of his own hands, something tucked in between his fingers. There was a rapid exchange, and the lowlife was scurrying off with an almost ecstatic expression on his ravaged face.

"If we can git past that injun, we can sneak down that alley and see if we can rustle up something from the bins out back," Bart whispered

to Nate and Anna.

They continued to watch the two-headed indian. Every few minutes a different hobo wandered up to him and purchased something off him. What, the three kids had no idea. From their vantage point, they could only see a rapid flicker of fingers and a brief glimpse of something wrapped in paper.

Eventually they decided to cross the road further down. Slowly, casually, they sauntered closer. Another badly-dressed customer approached, but this one seemed a bit more lucid and wanted to haggle. While the indian was conducting business, the kids finally managed to dart past him and down into the alleyway.

But while the indian's right head continued with the transaction, his left head spotted the movement out of the corner of one eye. He turned and saw the trio scamper down the alleyway past him. He gave a thin, cruel half-smile.

It was about time they took the bait.

* * *

In the yard connecting both the tavern and bakery, the children found some mouldy hardtack and beef jerky in the bins, and gratefully hoed in. Bart was ravenous because he hadn't had anything for over twenty-four hours, and even Nate and Anna were grateful for the food. For a few minutes the children ate with relish, washing everything down with water from the pump at the centre of the yard.

But just as they were filling up, Nate noticed something moving out of the corner of his eye. It was a rope that appeared to be attached to something that had been spread out beneath them. As it drew into the air, he realised what it was: a net that had been concealed beneath the dirt and other detritus that had covered the floor of the yard. Nate had time for one catlike screech of warning before the thing was yanked up, high into the air. Bart cried in protest, and Anna gave an infuriated hiss. The giant net pulled up and captured the kids in its folds, a trap that had obviously been set up a considerable while before.

Bart struggled to pull a pocket knife out to cut the rough thick rope, but the net was rocking so badly he lost his grip on it, and it slipped out through a hole and clattered to the ground about twelve feet below. Bart cursed in frustration. Anna, being thin and lithe, managed to slither out through another hole, but she didn't think she could drop such a distance without sustaining some broken ribs in the process. She slid out over the top of the net and started coiling her way up the rope to the pulley high above. However, the two boys were caught and swinging high in the air. While Bart cursed the loss of his knife, Nate started to gnaw angrily on the ropes, trying to chew out a larger hole.

A couple of two-headed indians stepped out from the back of the Sweet Sugar Shack. One tied the end of the rope fast around a hook that had been hammered into the wall. Both looked up at the kids with big smiles on their various faces. Then one noticed Anna perched on the pulley. Their smiles faded, and one unshouldered a bow. He nocked an arrow and aimed it at her. "Back in the bag before I skewer you, snake-girl," he growled.

Anna gulped. The Duoquois' aim was steady, and she didn't doubt he'd be able to hit her cleanly at twenty feet. Grudgingly, she slid back down into the net. The Duoquois cheered, and then a third indian appeared: the one from the front of the alley.

The Indian Giver rubbed his hands together with glee at the haul. Such unusual specimens would fetch a pretty penny at the underground slave-market. The next one would be taking place tonight—the youngsters would survive in the net until then. "But you better watch them—make sure the snake girl doesn't try to escape again," he told the man with the bow in their native tongue.

The bowman nodded, taking up a position beside the Sweet Sugar Shack doorway while the others went back inside.

The Duoquois were notorious slave traders. They preyed on runaway children such as these, drunks, and especially drug addicts. The dealer known as the Indian Giver had been doping unwitting victims for years, addicting them to Mescala worms. While the addicts were under the influence of the Perpetual Dream, they become easy pickings, unable to protest or even resist as they were dragged from the streets during the dead of night. They were taken into the back of the Sweet Sugar Shack, where a storeroom had been converted into a holding cell. Before they could sober up, they were taken down to the underground slave markets and sold to the highest bidder. By the time they returned to their senses, they were invariably miles away from Bhigge Smoche, chained together in a gang helping to excavate tunnels and mines, or imprisoned aboard a cart travelling to some gawdforsaken outland.

This was why so many of the city's homeless population were disappearing without trace. Nobody noticed or even cared what happened to the down-and-outs, and nobody missed them.

* * *

Nate peered nervously down through the thick strands of rope at the impassively-faced Duoquois standing below. At the moment only one head was watching them, but it was enough. The other was resting with its eyes closed. "What we gonna do now, Bart?" the cat boy asked nervously.

Bart gulped, struggling to find a solution. He was supposed to be the super-genius here. Surely he could come up with something? "Perhaps you could chew on a rope round the other side of the net, where he can't see you," he finally suggested.

"Yar." Nate wriggled around, changing position so he was behind Bart. He started to gnaw on the rope, but he was a cat, not a rat, and his teeth weren't designed for such hard work. He figured he'd be here for hours.

Suddenly Anna started to sing.

"What'choo doin' that for?" asked Bart in irritation. "This ain't the time nor place to be beltin' out a melody!'

Anna ignored him, continuing her song. It was a sad, soulful tale about a young woman whose lover had left her, and she threw herself from the top of a tower in despair. The glittering scales now almost completely covering Anna's body started to change colour in response, forming beautiful, hypnotic patterns. Tears stung Bart's eyes and Nate stopped his chewing to listen. Soon both boys were entranced.

Then Anna touched Bart with the tip of her tail, breaking the spell over him. Continuing her song, she used her tail to point down at the Duoquois.

He was standing, staring enraptured up at the net, with both heads. All four of his chocolate-brown eyes were wide and unblinking; he was completely spellbound!

Anna kept on singing, but in the words of her song she added a line of her own, commanding the indian to release them. Suddenly he moved, walking over to a corner of the yard where the rope holding them was tied. He undid it and slowly, mechanically, began to lower the net towards the ground.

"It's working!" Bart whispered excitedly to Nate.

The net landed with a thud. Hurriedly, Bart and Nate pulled the sides down and scrambled free. Bart scooped up his pocket-knife lying in the gutter. Anna continued her song as they hurried towards the pram they'd left near the mouth of the alley. Anna slithered inside and they took off for the main street at a run.

"That was amazing, Anna!" Bart gasped as soon as they were back on the main road, safe and surrounded by lots of people. "How'n hell you do that?"

"I dunno," said Anna. "Somehow I just knew what to do."

Bart experienced a flood of relief that Anna had finally come good and actually saved them from a fate that could, quite possibly, have been far worse than their prior life at the orphanage. "I'm glad you decided to come along with us," he told her.

"Me too," said Nate.

Anna gave them both a sweet smile. Then she adjusted her bonnet with her tiny hands, pulled her lipstick from her purse, and reapplied it. "Thank you. Now let's find where this dang sub's leavin' from!"

They headed off.

CHAPTER 16

As the sun was slowly rising over Mojo Town, it illuminated a forlorn figure trudging slowly and somewhat unsteadily up the steep slope of Boneyard Way. Zak had lost all of Sissy's money, his mechanical mule, his beloved cane, his favourite top hat, and even his clothing. He was wearing a battered wooden barrel to preserve his modesty, and his spindly legs poked out beneath. Starting midway on his thighs, both his limbs were completely mechanical, attached to his flesh with crude stitches. They were rusty, and held together in places with twine and baling wire. They creaked and groaned as he moved, because without pants to protect his legs, sand had gotten into their ancient joints.

Zak just wanted to collapse into his bed and sleep the sleep of the dead. But as he approached the orphanage, he noticed something that made him want to turn and run back into town as fast as his rickety artificial legs could carry him.

A large figure was sitting in a rocking chair on the sagging front veranda, moving gently back and forth. Sissy heard the grinding of his gears and looked up from her half-doze. She had something in one hand, which she slapped against the other with a loud whistle.

Zak gulped, realising he'd soon be wearing that riding crop around his shoulders. He didn't even want to think about how long he'd be in the doghouse this time, but where else could he go?

He clambered up the stairs and she rose to her feet.

He lifted his hands. "Sissy, hear me out! It wasn't my fault! I was swindled good an' proper by some smooth-talkin' lowlife card shark with gold teeth and fancy clothes! He was a lyin', cheatin' sonuvabitch snake who cheated me outta everything—"

"*You took all our life savings an' lost 'em drinkin' an' gambling!*" Sissy raised the riding crop threateningly. "An' no doubt there was a whore or two involved as well! Look at you! Standin' there in an awld barrel smellin' of fish! You're pathetic!" She brought the crop down, and he lifted his arms to protect himself. Still snarling and cursing, she whipped his arms and the barrel with a loud *thwack*.

Zak managed to stumble past her and blunder through the front door into the house. Sissy whirled around, trying to strike him on the backs of the thighs, but got him on the mechanical part of his legs, where he couldn't feel it. He ran for the stairs, hoping to maybe lock himself in his room until she cooled down in about a month or so.

Unfortunately, running up the steep, rickety old stairs dressed in a barrel proved a bit too difficult for his mechanical legs, and he slipped and started rolling backwards. Sissy, who'd just started charging up after him, had time for one shriek of horror before he crashed into her, knocking her back down the stairs and onto her titanic backside with a thunderous crash.

The barrel burst open, its wooden planks scattering everywhere. Zak managed to scramble to his feet and run for the stairs, butt naked.

"You even lost yer underwear?" Sissy threw off the pieces of barrel and lurched after him. "How'n tarnation could you lose yer underwear? Who'n hell would want your stained, holey ol' long johns?"

Zak raced into Bart's room, slammed the door, and tried to pull one of the boys' beds across to block it. But Sissy was a lot larger and stronger than he was, and still managed to shove the door open. The bed legs scraped across the floorboards as she forced her way into the little room. Zak shrieked and dived across the bed into the space behind it, ripping the blankets off in the process.

Still ranting, her face red and apoplectic with fury, Sissy leaned across the bed and raised her arm to whip Zak within an inch of his life. Zak yanked the blankets up over his head and started whimpering like a baby.

Then Sissy noticed something protruding from under Bart's pillow.

Zak, who'd been waiting for the riding crop, slowly, cautiously lowered the blanket to see what was going on. Maybe the old witch had finally had a heart attack and dropped dead. No, he definitely would have heard the thud of her huge body hitting the floor.

Sissy lowered her hand and reached for what was hidden under Bart's pillow.

Glad of the diversion, Zak asked: "Whatcha got there, Sissy?"

She drew out the old newspaper with the photo of the SandSub on the front. There appeared to be red crayon scrawled around the photo. No, it wasn't crayon; it was red lipstick. *Anna's* lipstick.

Sissy puts two and two together. "Tarnation, Zak! You know what this means?" She tapped the picture with a long, pointy fingernail. "Bart, Nate, and Anna weren't et by them zombie kids after all! Those sneaky li'l *bastards* used the diversion to run away!"

Slowly Zak picked himself up, holding Bart's blanket around his skinny body. "Yar, an' you wanna know what else? I don't think them kids risin' from their graves was an accident!"

"What'choo talkin' about, you thievin' fool?"

"Their graves 'ad been tampered with! A couple that hadn't risen had little funnels stickin' out of 'em. With *Stuff* 'round the edges! Bart did it. *Bart*! That sly li'l sonuvabitch!"

Sissy glared at him. "An' instead of comin' ta tell me, you stole all our money and practically *handed* it to the Watkins Corporation?"

Zak lifted a placating hand. "I'm sorry, Sis, but at the time I had no idea *what* I was lookin' at! Honest! Come—I'll show you. Just put that blasted crop away!"

She glared at him again, but then nodded. "Come on."

*   *   *

Because it took them the better part of a day to escape from the Duoquois slave traders, Bart, Nate, and Anna were forced to spend another night on the streets of Bhigge Smoche. This time Nate found them a balcony to sleep on, where they weren't disturbed, and he even brought Bart some stale rolls he found in a bin. Anna spent the entire night out by herself, hunting and working the kinks out from spending all her time curled up in the pram.

All three children were tired, hungry, and footsore when they finally arrived at the SandSub's docking port on the far edge of the city where the Scrubby Desert began. Sandy hills, occasionally pocked with boulders, patches of grass, and twisted trees, stretched off as far as the eye could see. The next town was at least 50 miles away, and beyond that a series of other towns. But far off to the south, at the bottom of the world, the Mighty Desert commenced, and out there *nothing* lived. And that's where the SandSub would travel in order to skirt around the Nogozo Canyon to reach Tutherside.

In reality, the *SS Desert Devil* was far larger and grander than the grainy black-and-white lumograph from Bart's newspaper. It stretched for hundreds of feet along the dock, sleek and as pale as the desert sand. There was a soft rumble from its engines, and puffs of smoke emerged from the tall chimney at its back. Brightly-coloured bunting stretched from it to the periscope at the front.

Three gangplanks ran from the dock across to large round doorways in the sides of the SandSub, and grandly-dressed passengers glided haughtily aboard. A huge crowd had gathered on the dock to farewell their relatives and see the sub off. Off to one side a big brass band was playing cheerful oompah music, and several tents and stalls had been set up, selling SandSub souvenirs. Clowns, acrobats, contortionists, and freaks entertained the crowds, and balloon-sellers loudly hawked their wares. Streamers and ticker tape floated through the air, falling down on the sub and the sand below.

Bart and Nate pushed the pram to a stop behind one of the tents and changed out of their now rather grubby dressing-gowns into their Sunday best. Nate pulled on gloves and a hat and wrapped a scarf around the lower part of his face, hiding his catlike features. Anna donned her prettiest bonnet and her biggest bows. Then she slipped a long cloak around her snakelike body.

"What're you doin'?" asked Bart. "Get in the pram!"

"No, I'm sick of that stoopid baby thang. In this cloak I look just like one o' those bendy acrobats."

"She does," agreed Nate.

"Yar, but you'll attract too much attention. We're trynna be *sneaky*."

Anna opened her mouth to retort, and then realised he was right. She stuck her tongue out. "*Fine.*" Abandoning the cloak, she slithered back into the pram. The boys neatened up her blankets and tucked her back in.

Bart slicked back his hair and also put on a hat. Then he checked out their outfits. "Now we look like someone's kids instead of a group o' waifs."

"How we gonna get aboard?" asked Nate.

"Come on—let's get a bit closer." Bart led them over to a large pile of suitcases still waiting to be loaded, and parked the pram. One of the gangplanks was only a few feet away. At the top, a queue of people were greeted by a clockworker dressed in smart red livery with shiny brass buttons. It was taking tickets, then waving the passengers along with a big fake smile on its silk-covered face. But then a large woman in a furry stole handed over her ticket, and the clockworker's artificial grin faded. "This is a *child's* ticket, ma'am," it told her. "You need an adult one."

"It most certainly is not!" the woman blustered. "I paid full price for that, and an exorbitant sum it was, too!"

While the woman argued with the machine, its entire attention was on her, and several passengers who'd become annoyed with waiting simply pushed their way on board and disappeared inside.

"There's our chance! The clockworker can't focus on more'n one at a time!" Bart started pushing the pram towards the gangplank. Nate followed, and they joined the general crowd waiting to file aboard. The clockworker ended the argument by ripping up the woman's ticket, throwing it in her face, and telling her pointedly to get another one.

"I have *nevah* been so shabbily treated!" she shrieked. "The Watkins Corporation will certainly hear about this!"

Three more people managed to push their way on board as the irate woman turned and shoved her way back down the gangplank. Then the clockworker managed to grab hold of a fourth passenger and spun him around with its superior strength. "Ticket, please!"

The man yelped and held it out in a shaking hand. The crowd continued to shuffle forward. Then a group containing six children held up the line as the clockworker counted each one. Four more passengers slid past while it was focussed.

Nate gulped. "I dunno if I can do it, Bart. I don't like that clockworker thang. Its eyes are dead and it smells funny. Like an old sofa someone spilled oil on."

Bart patted Nate's shoulder. "I'll go first. Watch how I sneak past it, then you follow." But then he paused and looked down at Anna. "But how we gonna get you on board without raisin' eyebrows?"

Anna slithered partway out of the pram. "Don't worry about me. I'll find my own way on board. You can leave the stoopid thang behind."

"Awright," said Bart. He collected his rucksack from the pram and started manoeuvring his way casually through the crowd on the gangway. One moment he appeared to belong to one couple, then the next moment he was tagging along behind some other adults. Each time he moved, he made sure the clockworker's attention was focussed directly on the person in front of it. He did this until he reached the top. As fortune would have it, a very large man in a suit several sizes too small paused to show his ticket to the clockworker, and Bart managed to slide in behind him and onto the sub. He disappeared through the big round doorway.

Nate squinted. "I don't see him no more. Where is he?"

Anna pointed a tiny arm to a small speck waving excitedly from one of the windows. "Up there! Now's your chance, Nate!"

Nate gulped again. "Awright. Now I guess it's our turn." He looked down at the pram, but it was empty. Anna had already slithered off. He squinted through the people's moving legs, trying to spot her, but she could have slipped underneath the gangplank and be slithering in that way.

Nate's heart started to race. He grabbed his bag from the pram and started to slide his way up onto the gangplank. He tried to copy Bart's movements, but even though he was very agile, he wasn't nearly as adept at avoiding the clockworker's attention. As he tried to slip aboard behind a woman in a large hat covered with flowers and fake fruit, the automaton snaked out an arm and caught him by the collar.

"Ticket, please!" it demanded.

"Um … er … I'm sorry … uh, sir, but me family's awready aboard! They got me ticket! We was separated."

The clockworker stared intently at him. Nate couldn't see any humanity in its jewel-like eyes, and its strange smell was so strong to his sensitive cat's nose that it was almost sickening. He wanted to scream and attack the vile thing with his teeth and claws, rip all that fake padding off it. He didn't know how people could stand the things. "You were trying to sneak aboard," the machine declared. "Now leave!" It was about to push him back down the gangway when a voice from within the sub's big round doorway called his name.

"Nate! *There* you are! Thank goodness! Thank you *sooo* much for finding him, Mr Clockworker, sir!" Bart reached out, grabbing Nate by an arm. "Pa's been lookin' *everywhere* for ya'. He's in his cabin. Yer gonna get a whipping this time, trying to run off like that!"

Cocking its head to the side, the clockworker appeared satisfied and released Nate, directing its attention to the next person in line.

Bart hurried Nate into the area where he'd waved from: a large observation deck with a shiny wooden floor. It was lined with portholes, and crowded with people waving to those down below on the wharf. "Thank goodness for that! Now all we hafta do is wait for Anna. Hopefully she'll give us some sign she managed to git aboard without attractin' too much attention to herself." He led Nate over to one of the windows.

It was so noisy and crowded on the observation deck that the boys didn't even notice the raised voices until someone called out: "That's them over there!"

Bart and Nate spun around to the horrible sight of fat Aunt Sissy and skinny Uncle Zak standing with a tall sheriff. She wore a big hat and had a big yellow star on her chest. Her name tag read "Shania Law".

Bart felt like someone had just removed the base of his stomach, and everything inside was plummeting to the floor. His knees felt like water. He wanted to collapse. All that planning, that enormous journey, the hardships they'd endured ... *all for nothing*.

Sissy, looking a little haggard and wispy from twelve hours on the trackless train, planted her hands on her ample hips and glared at the boys with her brows lowered and fanglike teeth bared.

"Oh no, sprung!" Nate burst into tears.

"How did you find us?" Bart finally managed.

Suddenly Sissy's long skirt moved, and a very familiar face peered out from underneath. Anna, still in her fanciest bonnet and bows, clutched at Sissy's skirt with her little atrophied arms.

The big sheriff and Zak stepped forward. Bart wondered if he ought to make a run for it. Maybe he could lose himself in the crowds! But then the sheriff grabbed him by an ear and dragged him over to Sissy. Zak had caught hold of Nate.

"Perhaps a night in the hoosegow might teach these delinquent runaways a lesson," Sheriff Law declared.

Suddenly Sissy's scowl transformed into an expression of joy. As though she'd turned on a tap, tears started to stream down her weathered face. She dropped to her knees with a loud thud and bear-hugged both boys to her enormous bosom. Bart cringed and wished that he had a pistol so he could end it all.

"Oh, my dear, sweet boys! I was so worried about you. I'm so glad yer safe. Please don't scare me like that again. I don't know what I'd do if something happened to ya. I jus' couldn't live with m'self!"

Almost suffocated against the mothball-smelling lace of her straining bodice, the boys were unable to respond. Bart continued to wish he was dead. Nate closed his eyes and tried not to breathe in too deeply.

Nate managed to twist his head and look down at Anna with a furious glare. Anna, still hiding under Sissy's voluminous skirts, beamed him a beatific smile, as though butter couldn't melt in her gigantic expanding snake-mouth.

Nate mouthed a single word at her: "*Traitor.*"

Completely unrepentant, Anna continued to smile, flickering her little forked tongue at him. Then she disappeared back under Sissy's skirts.

Sissy straightened up, grasping each boy by the wrist in her firm,

147

gnarly hands. "Thank you, Sheriff Law," she told the enforcer. "We will always be eternally grateful for your help in finding our poor lost children."

Sheriff Shania Law tipped her ten-gallon hat. "Glad to be of service, ma'am. Now take care of these rapscallions, you hear? Don't ever wanna see their faces on a wanted poster."

Sissy smiled. "No fear of that, Sheriff. I'm sure these two will be perfect angels from now on." Making sure her grip on Bart's and Nate's arms was secure, she marched them from the SandSub's observation deck towards the exit. Zak followed, swinging a new-looking cane with a silver knob on the end. As they stepped out onto the gangplank, there was a loud cheer from the crowds assembled on the dock below, and a great cloud of confetti erupted as everyone threw up their hands in celebration.

The clockworker in the doorway tipped his hat, and as soon as Sissy, Anna, Zak, and the boys had stepped from the gangplank, two wharfies darted forward to remove it and carry it away. The other gangways were also taken down, and ropes were yanked from the SandSub's sides and hauled back into the dock.

Even Sissy and Zak turned to watch the magnificent craft's departure, although they kept a good hold of Bart and Nate, just in case they tried to escape again.

The sleek vessel's engines, which had been rumbling at a soft idling pace, began to accelerate. The small puffs of smoke from the rear chimney became a steady stream of thick sooty blackness. The sand surrounding the sub began to ripple and become fluid. Small rocks disappeared beneath the surface. People at the windows and on the deck smiled and waved frantically before filing below. Then, in a grand display for the audience, the SandSub slowly sank beneath the surface. Fine sand sprayed from the rear of the device, showering those unlucky enough to be standing at the very edge of the dock.

The sub descended into the sand until only the periscope and chimney were protruding. Then it started to move off, slowly at first, then with increasing speed until it was travelling faster than the trackless train, almost as fast as Bart's speed-buggy had. The decorative bunting attached to the periscope and funnel snapped, and then the machine was gone, disappearing in a mini-sandstorm to the south.

Nate continued to cry, but Bart just felt numb. He figured he would probably cry later, but right now he just felt dead inside.

"Awright, that's enough gawkin'." Sissy gave Bart's arm a painful squeeze. "We've gotta make the trackless train afore sundown."

They departed.

CHAPTER 17

Bart and Nate sat in the dickie seat at the back of a steam-driven wagon, facing backwards with their legs dangling, and watching the filthy, uneven cobblestones roll out from between the wagon's heavy disk wheels. They were on the way back to the trackless train depot at the centre of town.

"We could make a run fer it," suggested Nate. "I reckon we could escape into the crowds afore Aunt Sissy an' Uncle Zak even notice." He gestured towards the front of the wagon, where the Spindlers were seated behind the driver.

But Bart didn't even lift his head. "You might be able to get away, Nate. You're quick an' agile. You can survive on the streets by eatin' rats, and hide in places no one can reach. Some drunk tries to harass you, you kin just bite his face off. But I'll never make it." He waved a hand. "They'll just catch me."

Nate grabbed Bart's arm. "But I don't wanna go without you, Bart!"

"You should run from here, Nate. I'll only slow you down."

Nate gulped. He could see the truth in Bart's words. As a cat-boy, he had become something more than human, a creature equipped to survive in hostile environments. He scanned the crowds of people flowing around the wagon: revellers returning from seeing the SandSub off. Now he knew what he could do, he was confident enough, but he didn't want to do it alone. He squeezed Bart's arm again. "No, Bart, I'm not gonna leave you behind."

Finally, those tears Bart had been anticipating came. He sniffed and tried to hold them back, because he was a big boy and big boys didn't cry, but they refused to stop. Nate wasn't sure what to do; normally he was the one who cried, not big, strong Bart who'd always looked after him. Awkwardly he put his arms around his friend's shoulders and hugged him close, but that just made Bart cry harder.

All the traffic returning from the SandSub launch slowed the steam-wagon to a crawl, and Sissy kept screeching at the driver to move faster or they'd miss their train. With a curse, the driver yanked on the engine control reins and the wagon lurched forward, almost running over a young couple.

"Git outta the dang way, you dang fools!" Zak shouted at them, waving his cane menacingly.

As the couple stumbled past, glaring defiantly at the back of the vehicle, they noticed the two boys sitting on the dickie seat, one with his head down and the other comforting him. There was something odd about the second boy. He had a strange mark on his face.

A familiar wine-stain birthmark.

"Oh my goodness!" Louisa Bigelow gasped. "It's him! It's Nate!" She grabbed her husband's arm and squeezed it.

Jake, the burly factory-worker who'd saved her from her Mescala worm overdose, looked up just as another cart rolled past, blocking the wagon from view. "What? Your boy?"

"Yes! He was sittin' on the back of that wagon that nearly ran us over, with another boy!"

Jake blinked, but by the time another cart moved out of the way, the wagon was too far away for him to see who was sitting in the back. Just a pair of shadowy figures, who soon vanished into the crowds.

"But ... but you told me he was dead," Jake said gently. Sometimes his wife still had the occasional Mescala worm flashback.

"Yes, but I'd know that birthmark anywhere!" she insisted.

"And if he was alive, he wouldn't be much more'n a year old, would he? Just a baby, not a big boy capable of sittin' on the back of a wagon."

"But that mark! It was so clear on his face..." Louisa tailed off in confusion. Perhaps Jake was right. Perhaps she had only imagined it. "Damn it!" She slapped her forehead in a temper. "Wish I could stop seein' things!"

"The doctor said the visions would fade over time." Jake slipped an arm around her shoulders and hugged her tightly. "Come on—let's find somewhere nice for dinner."

*   *   *

Finally Bart managed to get his tears under control. He dragged an arm across his nose and lifted his head.

"Told yer we couldn't trust Anna," Nate said softly.

"Yar, we should've expected her to pull somethin' like that. I'll wager she saw Sissy an' Zak in the crowd, and decided to switch sides, show 'em where we were, so she wouldn't be punished. But like I said before, it's not her fault. Since she's a rattler, she can't help being a tattler." He smiled, hoping to cheer Nate up with the joke.

Nate lowered his gaze, slightly shamed, and then looked back into Bart's genial eyes. "Ya always seem to see the good in people. You're a good friend, Bart."

Bart felt a lump rise in his throat as more tears threatened to come, and was about to respond with something heartfelt when a pretty face in a flower-covered bonnet slid up over the back of the seat in front of them and swung around to face them.

Anna poked her forked tongue out. "You're a good friend, Bart!" she mocked in a soft, hissy voice.

Bart just sighed, but Nate bared his fangs at her and snarled in her face. Startled by his ferocity, she withdrew. "Bart may be a stand-up fella, but I'm a big angry *cat*, and one day I just might decide I feel like *snake* fer dinner!"

*   *   *

After a long, bumpy trip back to Mojo Town on the trackless train, Sissy, Zak, Bart, Nate, and Anna returned to the orphanage. Sissy had put the oldest children in charge during their absence, with the promise of good food and special privileges on their return. Thus the place was in relatively good order, not burnt to the ground or vandalised by ravenous children. Everyone was still alive, and even relatively uninjured.

Sissy allowed Nate and Anna to go to bed, but grabbed Bart by an ear and marched him down into the parlour. "You caused a lot of trouble here, boy. *A lot* of trouble. That stunt you pulled with those zombie children did a lot o' damage that you're gonna start repairin', as of tomorra."

Bart stared down at the toes of his shoes and said nothing.

"I know you ain't gonna run away again. I know that from now on you'll do as yer told, an' wots right by this family."

Bart kept his head down so she couldn't see his face: his narrowed eyes, the corner of his mouth raised in a sneer. Twelve hours on the trackless train with nothing to do but think had started his mind racing, thinking up new ways to thwart the miserable old harpy and her brother.

Sissy prodded him painfully in the chest. "Yer know how I know this, boy? Because I've figgered out yer weakness."

Bart froze in horror and looked up at her with incredulity, disdain, and contempt all mixed together.

She smirked and poked him again with her bony arthritic finger. This time she pushed it in hard. "You have a *heart*."

Bart gulped, realising that she was right.

"You might not care what happens to yerself, boy, but yer care about the others. An' if you do bad, I won't punish you. Oh no. I'll punish them instead. I'll punish *them* bad. Ya know I will."

Bart remembered what Nate had told him, that he could see the good in people. Well, right now he could see no good whatsoever in Sissy. She was like a demon in human form. But she could see right through him. He dropped his head again in defeat.

"I know ya understand, boy."

Oh, how he *hated* being called boy! But she knew that too, and used it to rile him and get under his skin.

"You think yer so smart, but the truth is written all over yer face! Yer just like one o' those books you love so much! Now git ta bed b'fore I slap—one of the others. Maybe Nate. Maybe give his furry little backside a good tanning! Wouldja like that? Ahahahaha!"

Bart couldn't bear anymore of Sissy's cruelty and turned away. The old witch's cackling laughter followed him like nightwings as he hurried upstairs to the little room he shared with Nate.

She'd won this battle.

* * *

And so the days began to drag on. Sissy made sure Bart was worked harder than ever before, and a close eye kept on him at all times. Sometimes Sissy watched him, sometimes Zak. Anna followed him around, sometimes surprising him when he least expected it by sliding down from a rafter above his head, or slipping out from under a bed to smile sweetly at him and flick her forked tongue in his face. To make matters worse, Sissy told all the other children that if Bart misbehaved, it would be they who suffered, not him, so this ensured they watched him like hawks, too. It also destroyed any trust they might have had in him, and they began to sneer at him when Sissy and Zak weren't watching: push him in the back, trip him, and be generally mean towards him. They knew he couldn't retaliate.

Only Nate stuck by him, and kept the worst of the teasing at bay with his sharp teeth and claws. Where once Bart had looked after him, he now felt he had to look after Bart. As Sissy's treatment of him finished its work, he became even more catlike, now more comfortable racing around on all fours, swishing his long tail to keep his balance. His fur grew thicker and covered him completely, save for the middle of his face, and he no longer needed to wear clothes. He didn't like anything restrictive on his body anymore. He could climb as agilely as a cat, see in the dark, and find his way around by smell.

Sissy didn't want to admit it, but he was by far her most successful project. Apart from Anna, none of her mutant children had taken to their new aspect so completely.

But their vigilance was unnecessary. Bart performed his duties mechanically, without protest, and to the best of his ability. He knew when he was beat, and wasn't about to attempt anything that would get the others punished, even if they had all turned against him. What precious little free time he did get, he spent in the library.

Days turned into weeks, and weeks into months. Slowly Sissy's plan came together. Everyone toed the line, including Zak.

Bart continued to do chores, including going down into the crater to gather the Stuff for their meals and Sissy's on-going experiments. He grew taller and stronger, but other than his extra fingers, he exhibited no further sign that the mutagenic material was affecting him. Anna grew even more snakelike, learning to control her hypnotic gaze, voice, and eyes to a phenomenal degree. She was able to wind all the others around her tail, save for Bart and Nate. Now that they knew what she was really like, they had become immune to her charms.

Other children also developed new talents. Spider Boy found he could create a form of silk from the Stuff flowing through his veins, and learnt to spin a web. He got in trouble when he cocooned Jarboy one evening, and kept him hanging from the ceiling all night. Holly and Ivy learnt to move as one, like they'd always been joined.

One evening Sissy came back from the Mojo Town markets with numerous bolts of colourful material. That night after dinner, she taught the children how to design and sew their own costumes.

"What we need these clown clothes for, Aunt Sissy?" asked Balloon Boy.

Aunt Sissy smiled and rubbed her bony hands together. "We, my children, are gonna put on a show. And what a show it'll be! A marvel of the ages that'll make us rich beyond our wildest imagining."

Bart, lurking in a corner with a broom, kept his head down and continued to sweep the floor.

Aunt Sissy snapped her fingers at him. "Bart! The blasted floor's clean enough! Git over here an' help with the cuttin'!"

As Bart moved to obey, Sissy continued to address the group. "It's bin almost a year since Uncle Zak lost all our money on the Watkins Desert-boat Zeppelin." She glared across the room at Zak, who was sprawled in an armchair with a newspaper in one hand and a glass of beer in the other. He pretended he wasn't listening. "If not for him, we'd a bin on the road months ago. But at least now we finally saved enough to get this show started." She rubbed her hands together again, then glared at Bart. "You call that cuttin'? I seen straighter dog legs!" She slapped the back of Holly's head instead of the boy's, and the girl snarled at him.

Bart cringed. "Sorry, Aunt Sissy—hard to use these scissors with six fingers."

"Don't wanna hear excuses, boy! This silk's expensive! Now straighten that up! My two Siamese darlings hafta look perfect!" She slipped her arms around Holly and Ivy's shoulders.

"Yes, Aunt Sissy." Bart trimmed the silk as carefully as he could. All the while Holly and Ivy glared at him, their hostile gazes threatening to bore through him.

* * *

A few days later, a loud roaring sound from the front of the house brought all the children rushing down the hall to see what was going on. "Hold on, hold on," Sissy growled as she lumbered ahead, and threw the front door wide.

Pulling in through the front gates of the orphanage was a long mechanical wagon in two parts, held together by a pivoting joint in the middle so it could manoeuvre around corners more easily. It was battered and filthy, the funnel at the front spewing out far more thick black smoke than it should have. Several panels were missing, revealing sections of engine, and the wheels were dented and crooked.

Aunt Sissy put her hands on her hips and sniffed in disdain. "This the best you could get? What a clapped-out pile o' junk!"

"Come now, Sissy," Zak jumped down from the driver's seat, which looked like it had been eaten by rats in places. "You know such vehicles are expensive! I was lucky ta get this one! The dealer was gonna sell it to someone over in Rancid Falls!"

Sissy sniffed. "I'm sure you got royally swindled, as per usual! That ugly ol' thang looks like it's gonna fall apart any minute!"

"All it needs is some oil an' a lick o' paint!"

"Awright." Aunt Sissy turned to the children, who'd all clustered behind her. Her predatory eyes fell on Bart. She pointed. "An' I know just the fella who ken help. Go out there an' git started!"

"Yes, Aunt Sissy." Keeping his head down, maintaining his subdued, beaten-down appearance, Bart shuffled out. But truthfully, he was excited for the first time since his return from Bhigge Smoche.

He couldn't *wait* to get started on fixing that old articulated wagon. He wondered what would happen if he poured some Stuff into the engine…

No! He had to shake his head to clear it of the tempting thought. No experiments, nothing that would get anyone in trouble. *Just keep yer head down and do the dang job properly*, he told himself.

But of course, Bart couldn't do such a big chore on his own. While he pulled apart, cleaned, and oiled the engine, Zak pulled out the damaged seats and cut new planks for them. Spider Boy, Nate, and Stilts—the lad with the long thin legs—scrambled around the outside, cleaning off the rust and then painting it in bright colours. Anna, who could now manoeuvre into the smallest of spaces, slithered through the contraption looking for hidden damage.

Aunt Sissy watched the conveyance slowly transform, and couldn't keep a smile of satisfaction from her thin, cruel lips. What she had come to think of as Zak's latest Big Mistake might actually be transformed into a vehicle worthy of carrying them all around the countryside. "I gotta admit that's startin' to come along real nice."

Zak straightened with a creak of his mechanical legs. "Yar. We're gonna knock 'em dead."

Nate couldn't read or write, so Spider Boy and Stilts painted on the side of the wagon in garish multi-coloured letters: *Spindler's Sensational Sideshow*!

CHAPTER 18

Sissy couldn't believe her senses. It was happening at last, at long, long last! Her grand plan, which she'd been working on since she'd discovered the wonders of the Stuff and how it affected the children placed in her care, was finally in motion. She was as excited as a schoolgirl and couldn't stop darting around like a very, *very* large hummingbird, making sure everything was taking place to her satisfaction.

At her tallboy, she pulled out her clothes and undergarments and stuffed them into a carpetbag. She also packed her treasured waterglobe with the beautiful little house called "Rosewell". The trinket was her lucky charm. It had survived so many years. It would help her to survive many more and keep her dreams alive. Never mind that her dreams, for many, had turned into twisted nightmares.

* * *

The articulated wagon was finally ready, and Zak, Bart, and the mutated children spent the better part of a day loading it with a colourful marquee, camping equipment, rucksacks full of clothing, lamps, trail rations, canned food, dried meat from all the farm animals that had been recently killed and cured, waterbags, and everything else they would need for their first grand tour.

Even though Bart maintained his constant dour demeanour, he had to admit he was excited by the thought of finally getting away from the grim old orphanage. He'd already installed his bag for the trip, and it contained a notebook he'd found in the library, where he hoped to start documenting everything new he discovered on the way. He was even thinking about writing everything down from his Bhigge Smoche trip. Long journeys without much to do would give him ample opportunity to pen his thoughts.

The sun set, and the last of the supplies were stowed aboard. Sissy called everyone back into the orphanage for the evening meal. All the children hoped this would be the last night of her disgusting, tasteless gruel.

"Is the tent an' all its gear loaded?" Sissy asked Zak. "The pegs, poles, mallets, an' all the ropes?"

Zak rolled his eyes. "Yar, Sis. They were the first things we put on board.

Sissy refused to be mollified. Zak couldn't organise a booze-up in a brewery at the best of times without her help. "What about all th' costumes?"

"Yup. Every single one."

Sissy rattled off a few more things, and Zak answered in the affirmative each time. She glared at him. "You've been mighty well-behaved lately, brother dear, an' it's makin' me suspicious."

Zak looked like butter wouldn't melt in his mouth. "Just trynna make up for losin' all that cash on the Desertboat."

"I find *that* hard ta believe," she grumbled. "Yer definitely up ta somethin'."

After the evening meal, Bart helped to clean up and wash the dishes. When he finished, around nine o'clock, his exhaustion from the day of packing got the better of him, and he started to shuffle from the kitchen, thinking only of washing and collapsing into bed.

"An' where do ya think yer goin', Barton?" Sissy called.

Bart froze in the doorway, his blood running as cold as ice water. Had he forgotten something? "Um, to bed?"

"Don't be a smart-mouth, Bart. Yer ain't finished yer chores yet."

Slowly, Bart turned around, at his wits' end. "But I've washed all the dishes, dried an' put 'em away, swept the floor, tidied up... What else? What else could there *possibly* be fer me ta do, other than drop dead from exhaustion?" He flung up his hands in exasperation, only after his comment remembering that one of his fellows was probably going to get smacked for it.

But Sissy just grabbed him by an ear and hauled him upstairs. When she dragged him into her bathroom, he realised with dismay what she wanted him to do. Surely this horrible job could wait? But no, tomorrow they'd would be on the road. "Aw, no," he groaned before he could stop himself.

"Enough o' that. I need you to concentrate. Don't want you cuttin' me again." She slipped out of her huge, billowy housedress and started undoing her enormous industrial-strength corset.

Bart cringed at the sight of all the growths that had returned since the last time he'd been forced to perform this grisly job a few months earlier. They were even larger than before. Some actually looked like twisted, atrophied legs, with mangled feet and toes at the end. Bart's stomach performed a lazy roll and he had to gulp to keep from vomiting.

"What's the hold-up back there?" Sissy demanded. "Git 'em off! They're really startin' to chafe under me smalls!"

'Smalls' is hardly the word I'd use to describe your humungous undergarments, Bart thought as he selected a scalpel and started to slice into the first of the weird little limbs.

"Make sure you git 'em as close to the skin as possible—not *that* close, you careless little sod!"

"Sorry, Aunt Sissy." Bart sliced off another, trying to be as precise as she wanted. The cuts oozed blood, but quickly healed. He continued working. Because he became quicker and more adept each time he removed Sissy's growths, it only took him an hour to clear them all from her body. But then, as he was removing the last one up near the back of her neck, he thought about whipping the scalpel across her throat again. He was getting pretty handy with the thing.

He narrowed his eyes. No, unless he could somehow cut her whole head off in one go, it wouldn't work. He still had no idea how fast her regeneration was.

"Hurry it up back there! Some of us need our beauty sleep!"

Bart collapsed into bed at about eleven o'clock. But what felt like only a few hours later, Sissy was flinging open the door and ringing a little bell. "Come on, babies, rise an' shine!"

It wasn't even light yet. Bart cursed and flung off the blankets. He roused Nate, who came awake with a loud meow of protest and a flail of bad-tempered claws at being disturbed. Bart only just managed to dodge in time. Sissy laughed.

"Sorry, Bart!" Nate gasped.

"Stow it and move yer lazy behinds!" Sissy growled, and lumbered off to rouse the rest of the young'uns.

After a hasty breakfast, the children filed up into the wagon train. Zak had woken early to fill the boiler, stoke the fires, and get the engine up and running. Now it hummed smoothly, and the smoke that puffed from its chimney came out steadily and cleanly, without any sparks or soot. Bart had done a magnificent job of getting it working at peak efficiency.

"Everyone in the wagon!" Sissy shouted. "Chop chop! C'mon, squeeze in, squeeze in! Plenny o' room up the back."

There would have been more room, but half of the first part of

the wagon was taken up with the private compartment Sissy had arranged for Zak and herself, complete with comfortable beds, curtained windows, storage areas, and portable commodes. Sissy immediately climbed into her bed and made herself comfortable.

"No one make a sound 'til I wake up, ya hear?" she barked at the kids all squashed in on the hard benches behind her. She pulled a sliding door across with a slam.

"No, Aunt Sissy!" the children chorused.

Clutching his notebook and wearing a wide-brimmed hat, Bart clambered up beside Zak in the driver's seat.

"No, you git in the back with the others!" Zak barked at him.

Bart gave Zak what he hoped was his most obsequious smile. "Uncle Zak, I pulled apart that whole engine an' cleaned every gear an' cog—I know exactly how it works. I ken help you drive if you git tired, and fix up anythin' that breaks."

Zak glared at him. Then he smiled and tugged at his thin, twisted beard. "Good idea! I'm still pretty beat from yest'day, an' I could use a rest. Awright, I'll git us goin', and then you ken take over once Aunt Sissy wakes up. Can't have you drivin' unsupervised. You might take us all over a cliff or somethin'."

Bart saluted. "Yes, sir."

Their tour would take them through all the small towns along the trackless train route to Bhigge Smoche, and after a tour around the big city they'd return home, hopefully with enough money to upgrade the wagon. After a period back at the orphanage, while Sissy developed some new and more interesting mutants, the show would start again.

The journey commenced. Unfortunately, because the vehicle rose on thin disks instead of fat wheels or wide tracks, progress was slow and bumpy. The metal wheels slipped on the sand, bounced off rocks, and skidded every which way. Bart honestly had no idea how fast they were going, but he figured it was no more than half of the trackless train's average speed. His speed-buggy would have left this antiquated contraption for dead.

Zak drove for about five hours before Aunt Sissy finally woke up and demanded to know what Bart was doing up front with him. Fortunately the boy's suggestion was actually quite logical, and she agreed to let him stay and drive while Zak scrambled gratefully into the little cabin and promptly fell asleep.

Sissy clambered up beside Bart, grumbling at the effort it took to wedge her mighty bulk into the hard, narrow seat. "How'n hell can he sit up here?" she complained. "This is hardly a seat at all! More like a ledge."

"I dunno, Aunt Sissy," said Bart, although a thousand more snide retorts were warranted.

"I think you're goin' a bit too fast there! Slow down!"

"Yes, Aunt Sissy."

"An' move over a bit. Yer right in the middle of the road. What if a wagon comes the other way? It'll plough right into us!"

"Yes, Aunt Sissy."

"Why's it so bumpy? Dang it! We're ridin' on sand, but my behind feels like it's gonna fall off!"

"I don't know, Aunt Sissy."

"What was that? Was that some sorta lizard? You almost hit it!"

"No, Aunt Sissy. I missed it."

"Ugh! (cough, splutter) I think I just swallered a bug!"

"I'm sorry about that, Aunt Sissy. They's a lotta bugs out here."

"It's awful hot. Stop while I go back an' git myself a hat."

"Yes, Aunt Sissy."

"Why we slowin' down? We there yet?"

"No, Uncle Zak. Go back ta sleep."

Bart couldn't believe how much he was enjoying this. He felt like he'd just received a new lease on life. It wasn't just the chance to see Aunt Sissy and Uncle Zak so uncomfortable and out of their element, but the chance to get out and see the world. Previously, driving the speed-buggy, he'd been so preoccupied with escape that he hadn't paid a lot of attention to his surroundings, or appreciated the difference of the world outside the orphanage. But now every new sight imprinted itself upon his mind, and he vowed to keep a record.

The trackless train, on its way to Mojo Town, thundered past them during the mid-afternoon, showering them with dust and sand and creating a great cloud that refused to settle.

* * *

As the sun sank towards the dusty horizon, Sissy decided that she'd had enough of all the rattles and bumps of the road, and that it was time to stop for the night. She spotted a nice flat patch of ground in the shadow of a large rock, surrounded by low, dried-out scrub and dead trees. She ordered Bart to park and cut the engine. Then she jumped down, almost falling flat on her face in the process because her legs were so stiff, and clapped her hands for everyone to emerge and start setting up the campsite. She ordered Zak to dig a fire pit, while Bart and Nate were to go out and fetch some wood.

As the boys were searching, they noticed some ancient stone ruins protruding from the sand around the edges of the flat patch. Bart wondered if an entire ruined city from another era lay hidden down there.

The tired children quickly set up a temporary camp amongst the ruins, consisting of various hoochie tents. Anna slithered around these crude accommodations, turning her nose up in disdain, and then slid back into the wagon to curl up under a seat.

Sissy placed a cauldron in the fire to heat up some of the meat they'd packed. The children enjoyed a campfire meal that, for once, wasn't tainted by her ever-present Stuff gruel. Never had salt pork, beans, skunk eggs, grits, and stale Johnny cakes tasted so good! The kids gobbled down their meals in seconds flat, and Spider Boy had the audacity to signal for more. Sissy was so aghast she didn't know what to do, and smacked Bart in the back of the head before she realised she'd gotten the punishment completely ass-about.

"What was that for?" Bart complained.

Sissy pointed a quivering finger. "You! Sentry duty! Now!"

It figures, Bart thought darkly. *Lucky I don't need more'n a few hours' sleep per night these days.* While the other children all settled down in their hoochie tents, and Sissy and Zak retired to the wagon, Bart wandered to the edge of the clearing, where a dead sapling stood. He cut it down with his pocket knife and sharpened the end. Then he took it to the fire and turned it around in the flames a few times, hardening the tip. He wanted a weapon in case they were attacked by werecoyotes.

Although he doubted a pointy stick would have much effect on a werecoyote. Those "Dogs o' War", as they were called, were nigh on indestructible when they decided a feast lay in their path. If a group decided they were fair game, nothing would save them.

Bart settled down with one of the dead trees at his back, his makeshift spear across his knees and his notebook close at hand. From his vantage point he could see most of the campsite, still illuminated by Zak's flickering fire. He heard the soft pad of a foot nearby and immediately snatched up his weapon, pointing it at a very surprised Nate.

Bart laughed. "Sorry, Nate! I's put on watch! I gotta be alert, an' you're very quiet."

Nate sat down beside Bart. "I tried ta be as loud as possible, but I'm naturally quiet now." He flicked his tail around his body, perched as neatly as any cat beside his friend. "So whatta we lookin' out for? Bandits?"

"Naw, werecoyotes."

Nate pricked his ears up. "Werecoyotes? What're they?"

Bart explained all about the Dogs o' War. Nate's glowing eyes grew wider and wider as the flames of night slowly died down. "Surely not!"

"'Fraid so. Those ravenous monsters keep things int'resting out here at night. Not sure if Aunt Sissy an' Uncle Zak thought things through.

But we're 'ere now, an' we gotta do the best we can."

Nate made sure all his claws were strong and sharp. "I reckon I could give those mangy dogs somethin' ta think about." He stretched out on a large flat rock beside Bart and stared up at the clear, dark night sky. It was never this pristine in Mojo County. "What d'you think might be up there, Bart? Whatta you read about them little twinklin' lights in them books o' yours?"

Bart squinted up at the strange little points of light in the sky. "I read many theories about 'em, but none I truly believe. Some reckon the dark sky is a curtain that's pulled across at night, an' the white dots are holes in it … others say the dots are the spirits of our ancestors, lookin' down on us an' keepin' us safe."

Nate blew a raspberry.

Bart laughed. "Yar, no one is keepin' us safe save *us*. Now, there's a scientician from Bhigge Smoche who reckons those lights are gigantic balls of gas, billions o' miles away and many thousands o' miles wide, burnin' away like fires bigger'n the whole West itself."

Nate blew an even louder raspberry. Bart laughed again. "Ayuh, that does sound far-fetched, all right. Though the truth is probably much, much stranger. "There are scienticians that reckon those lights are little gaps created when our universe bumps into the next one along."

"What?" gasped Nate.

"All the realms in existence are like big balloons, an' when they touch each other, they join together for a little while. Stuff can pass through."

"Stuff?" asked Nate. "Like the Stuff Aunt Sissy uses on us?"

Bart opened his mouth to answer, and then paused. "I just meant stuff in general. But I never thought about where the Stuff in the crater might actually have come from. You could be right. It could come from outside. From some other realm. Or maybe from someplace in between the realms, where there's nothin' but chaos."

"Whoa," said Nate, his eyes wide. He wasn't sure how to respond to that. Sometimes his friend seemed to have access to knowledge so far beyond his ken that it seemed almost unreal. His brain never focussed on things like that. These days he mostly thought about food. It seemed no matter what he ate, he was always hungry.

Suddenly, from off in the distance came a long, eerie howl. Bart tightened his grip on his spear and Nate hissed, flattening his cat-ears against his skull.

"Don'tchoo worry about them," said Bart, relaxing. "They's miles away. Sound always does weird things in the desert."

Unfortunately, werecoyotes were the least of their problems.

CHAPTER 19

For a while, Bart and Nate stayed awake together, Bart making notes in his diary and Nate occasionally asking questions. Both looked up every few minutes or so to make sure nothing was creeping in towards the camp. Nothing was, but danger could come from all directions.

Eventually Nate fell asleep beside Bart, and the older boy put down his spear and got up. He patrolled around the camp a few times, and then returned to the rock to continue watching. But his day of driving eventually caught up with him, and he could no longer keep his eyes open. Sissy hadn't arranged a relief for him, and he succumbed to sleep at around midnight.

Not long after this was when the intelligent stalker decided to make its move. Under one of the hoochie tents, the sand began to ripple, and a giant pair of glossy brown nippers slid out, grabbed one of the sleeping children and pulled it under the surface. Before the child realised what was going on, it had been smothered and eaten. The other three children who'd been sleeping in the hoochie with the unfortunate victim didn't notice a thing.

Now whetted, the creature's appetite refused to be satisfied by one scrawny mutant kid. A few minutes later the sand rippled again, and the claws appeared around the body of a second child in a different hoochie tent. This time the movement of the sand around the child's bedroll woke him, and he blinked to see a pair of sharp, evil-looking pincers snapping closed around his midriff.

The mutant quadruped boy, known as Rex, had time for one warning howl before those claws crushed his ribs and lungs and knocked all the air from his body. He was yanked down through the still-rippling sand and devoured.

Bart leapt to his feet, brandishing his spear. Nate came awake with a yowl and sprang onto all fours, claws out, teeth bared.

Now the predator was *really* hungry. It couldn't remember the last time it had tasted such a succulent feast of soft flesh. It wanted *more*.

The time for subtlety was past. It had an ability to blow air through the sand so it became fluid, like quicksand. Now it used that talent to rise bodily to the surface: a giant, 12-foot semi-humanoid crab hermit with one hand and one enormous claw that immediately reached for another victim.

But by now, most of the children had woken up and were scrambling to their feet in terror. Some were able to escape right away, but others weren't so lucky. The mutant crab-monster's eyes on stalks focussed on one child, who'd had all the bones dissolved from his body and could only ooze slowly along the ground like a flatworm. Those fearsome nippers closed around him. A triangular mouth filled with needle-sharp teeth opened in anticipation.

With a shriek he hoped would distract the beast, Bart leapt at it and jabbed his spear at its midriff. But like a crab, it had developed a hard chitin coating, and the flimsy wooden spear skidded off its armour. Its hand swung almost casually, sending Bart flying. The nippers lifted the boneless child high into the air and cut him in half. His rubbery upper torso dropped into that huge triangular mouth, where those numerous teeth immediately and hungrily masticated it into mush.

The monster scooped up the rest of the body with its other hand and crammed it into its enormous mouth. Chewing vigorously, still not satisfied, the ravenous beast directed its attention to the next tasty morsel. Children were running hither and thither, some screaming, others crying. Several clambered up into the caravan for safety. But one had frozen in fear.

Nate could stand up to humans all right, but he had never seen such a horror before in his life. Right now he could only stare and mouth silently. The thing seemed to be the stuff of his worst nightmares.

The crab monster approached, nippers snapping in anticipation.

Bart scrambled to his feet, snatched up his spear, and leapt into the path of the giant crab hermit. This time, as he focussed on it, he noticed that its armour didn't cover it completely. There were soft spots in between the plates, allowing it to move. All he had to do was find the right soft spot in its underbelly.

As the thing charged towards him, deciding that Bart would be its next meal, he thrust his spear up as hard as he could at the precise moment the monster sprang. He managed to jam its point into the gap between the beast's chest and stomach-plates. For one horrible moment he thought the spear was going to splinter against its armour. But then, after a brief pause, it slid easily into the soft meat beneath and pierced the creature's heart.

The giant crab hermit froze, and an expression that could only be described as abject horror crossed its face. Its eyes stood straight out from its head, and its triangular mouth opened in a final roar of despair. The spear shuddered in Bart's grip as the monster's massive heart struggled to beat around it. Bart tightened his grip. Then the beast lurched forward, bringing its big claw up to try to snap the spear. Bart stumbled, but he managed to keep his hands around the shaft of his

weapon. He sat down on the sand and jammed the butt of the spear into the ground, bracing it as the monster fell to its knees and slowly began to slide down it. It managed to get its huge nippers around the spear, but by then all its strength had left it.

The spear-tip struck the underside of the armour on its back, and ever so slowly it keeled over and fell with a crash. Bart scrambled to his feet and jabbed it in a few more of its soft spots, making sure the creature was dead. Only then did he step back to catch his breath. Slowly, cautiously, Nate and the other children approached. Sissy, Zak, and Anna emerged last of all.

"We ... we lost Nobs, Rex, an' Boneless," Bart whispered, still in a state of shock. "This critter et 'em. But ... but I reckon if we boil him up, *he* will make good eating."

Sissy and Zak exchanged glances, and for once everyone agreed with Bart. The very next morning, everyone got to eat a delicious meal of boiled crab for breakfast, by far the tastiest meal everyone, including the Spindlers, had eaten.

Then they packed up and continued their journey. Bart fell asleep not long after the start, and not even the psychopathic Zak had the heart to wake him up. He was still too full and satisfied from one of the best meals of his life. He hadn't even eaten that well on the Watkins Desertboat.

It was around lunchtime that the first town on the trackless train route came into view, and Zak slowed the articulated wagon to a stop. He let Bart continue sleeping and jumped down.

Sissy emerged from the sleeping compartment. "Wot? Why we stoppin'?"

"We've reached Rancid Falls, Sis. First stop on our grand tour."

Sissy squinted at the distant buildings in disdain. "Let's hope those country-fried desert rednecks have some coin ta spend." She clapped her hands. "All right, everyone out! Time to set up the big tent!" She noticed Bart sleeping next to the driver's seat and shook him vigorously. "And you too, lazy bones! Just coz you killed one little crab-man doesn't mean you get ta sleep the whole day through!"

Still subdued from the tragedy the night before, everyone filed quietly from the caravan and began unloading.

Zak dug a fire-pit, ordered Bart and Nate to collect wood and find water, and then directed the rest of the children to start putting up the big marquee. The kids stumbled about, fell over the ropes, whacked each other with the mallets, and generally got in each other's way. They had no idea what they were doing, but Zak hoped in time they'd be able to work as a well-oiled machine.

Sissy sighed in exasperation at the ineptitude. "C'mon, children, shake a leg, get this blasted tent up. You'll have to work faster than this! We haven't got all day!"

But eventually, after a comedy of errors that would have made a fine clown show had anyone actually been watching, the big tent was up. It was red- and blue-striped, and looked quite impressive against the golden sand. But by this stage the sun had gone down, and everyone retired inside to rest. Since Bart had done such a good job the night before, he was put back on watch. Nate joined him, and this time they took turns so neither would be asleep at the same time.

The next day, while the children finished setting up the stage inside the tent, Sissy, Zak, and Bart—the three most normal-looking members of the group—went into Rancid Falls to put up some posters. The posters read "Spindler's Sideshow—Tonite Only at five o'clock—1 mile North. Adults $1, Children 50c."

"Ya don't think that's too cheap, do ya?" Zak asked Sissy.

"Of course it's too bloody cheap, but we gotta test the waters first. Besides, I doubt anyone in this filthy hickburg will be able to afford anymore'n that." She looked around at the ramshackle buildings in disdain. Most lining the main street were tumbledown and in bad need of repair. Only a few, such as the tavern and inn, looked like they had been taken care of. "A shame our first show's gotta be in a place called

'Rancid Falls'!"

"That's not the town's real name, Sis. The Rancid comes from some injun thang. Like Mojo's short for Mojohoke."

Sissy sniffed. "Ah, who cares? It smells bloody rancid here. Like a dead buzzard's armpit."

Suddenly Bart came running up, hot and out of breath. "There! That's the last of the posters, Aunt Sissy!"

"Good, let's git back an' wait for all the rubes, I mean, *customers* ta come rollin' in." She gave a wicked laugh.

* * *

Later that afternoon, Sissy pushed open the tent's front flap and peered out. She saw the crowds gathering on the ground outside. "They're startin' to come, Zak. You ready?"

Zak, dressed in a brand new top hat, tails, and tall leather boots, checked his outfit. He snatched up his cane and performed a few twirls with it. "Yar. How do I look?"

In his new hat and suit, armed with that cane, and his thin, straggly beard oiled and pulled into a neat curl, he looked every inch the ringmaster. But it had never been Sissy's job to massage anyone's ego. Pursing her lips, she planted her hands on her hips. After all, this was her inept clown of a brother she was talking to, and she hadn't come this far to be let down by a bad performance. "You remember howta do this, don't you?"

"Of course! Once a showman, always a showman. You know that, Sissy. Throwin' the bull is all I've ever bin really good at."

Sissy patted her new bonnet. It was covered with bows and ribbons. She ran her hands down her long pink dress. "How do I look?"

Like the Watkins Desertboat in a frilly tarp, Zak thought. "You look gorgeous, Sis. Now git out there an' make us some money!"

Sissy gave a girlish giggle and stepped out through the tent flaps.

The townspeople, who all looked like they'd just squeezed into their Sunday best, surged forward. "All right, all right! One at a time! One buck for adults, fifty cents for kids."

The excited people began to hand their cash over. "Go on in an' move all the way around," she ordered. "There's gotta be enough room for everyone!"

Sissy had a large pouch on her belt that she slowly began filling with notes and coins.

The people waiting to be allowed in started to bounce up and down in excitement, and Sissy caught snatches of their conversation:

"Gee, I ain't ever bin to a real sideshow b'fore."

"Ooh, I hope it ain't too scary."

"Don't you worry, Daizilou, it's just make-up and trickery."

Trickery, my eye, Sissy thought with a thin smile. She continued to take their money, and every so often checked the weight of her bag.

Inside the tent, the crowds started to gather. Zak stood on a large wooden stage in front of a big red curtain that shifted and pillowed as the performers hurriedly got ready behind it. Illumination was provided by various oil lamps hanging from the ceiling.

"Roll up, roll up, roll up!" Zak boomed in his best spruiking voice. It really was quite impressive, and managed to reach even those who were squeezing into the back. He flung his hands into the air. "Welcome to Spindler's Sensational Sideshow! The most incredible show in all of Westerillo!" Suddenly he stepped forward, craning towards the audience like he was about to impart a secret. "You are about to see wonders the likes of which have *nevah* been glimpsed in this world before! Fantastic beings! Genuine freaks! Critters that flout the very laws of nature themselves! You'll find no tawdry, stitched-together abominations here, my friends. All are one hundred percent *the real thang*."

The audience members gasped with excitement, captivated by his voice.

"And now, preee-senting, *Spindler's Sensational Sidehow!*"

Bart pulled on the curtain, and as it opened the boy hurled a smoke-globe. It shattered on the wooden stage in a small but impressive explosion of light and sound, revealing Anna in all her snake-like glory. She was dressed in her best bonnet, braids, and bows. She was even wearing her lipstick. Colours and patterns rippled across her beautiful scales.

Zak brandished his cane like a sword. "Be dazzled by the asphyxiating Python Girl!"

"Oh my goodness!" a woman exclaimed.

"Aww, she's not real. Jus' smoke and mirrors an' such!"

"No, my friend, she is *very* real!" Zak shouted as he walked all the way around her. "Allow me to present Bart, my trusty assistant."

Bart shuffled out from behind the curtain and took a bow. There was some giggling, as Sissy had decided he would look best in a sparkly red leotard.

"Anna, show all the doubters in the audience just how real you are."

Anna curled herself around Bart and held him tightly. Everyone gasped and clapped, even the naysayer. "Are you having as much fun as I am?" Anna whispered into Bart's ear.

Bart didn't bother dignifying that with an answer.

Anna opened her jaw, expanding her mouth as though to swallow Bart whole. Horrified gasps rippled across the audience at the sight of her enormous mouth and sharp teeth.

Zak laughed. "Now, now, Anna, no need to eat my assistant. Good ones are *sooo* hard to find. I have somethin' else for you, my dear." Zak leaned in behind the curtain, and one of the other children handed him a dead rabbit from the supplies.

Anna released Bart, and he shuffled back into position behind the curtain. Zak fed her the critter. There were more gasps and a few groans of disgust at the sight of the animal disappearing down her enormous mouth, and her throat working to push it into her stomach. Someone actually threw up.

"That's disgusting!" he croaked. Others were more grossed out by the puddle of puke on the floor, and struggled to move away from it.

"She's incredible!" someone exclaimed.

"She *is* incredible," boomed Zak. "But watch and wait—more amazing things are coming!"

Bart closed the curtain, and the next performer got into position. Anna slithered off to find somewhere nice and quiet to digest her meal.

"Allow me to present the next exciting exhibit—*the amazing Spider Boy!*"

Bart pulled the curtain and let off another smoke bomb.

Spider Boy appeared, dangling from the ceiling on a rope he'd made from his own Stuff. He glared at the audience through all eight of his beady little eyes.

There were more gasps and cries of alarm. "Ghastly!" someone cried.

Spider Boy swung down onto the stage and scuttled around to more exclamations of horror. He reared up on his back legs and menaced the people at the front with his forelimbs. He bared his long spider fangs in an evil hiss. "All right, Spider Boy, that's enough, that's enough. Stop hogging the show!" Zak laughed, and prodded Spider Boy in his enormous furry backside with the point of his cane. Spider Boy trudged off in a very obvious sulk, and Bart dropped the curtain.

"And now, preee-senting the Spindler Sideshow's very own exotic Siamese Twins, Holly and Ivy!" Another smoke bomb, and the curtain parted to reveal the girls, both heavily draped in gossamer veils. They appeared to be pressed back to back, and at the moment only their delicate bare feet could be seen, pattering across the wooden stage as they danced and gyrated to haunting music.

The audience clapped and cheered.

Behind the curtain, it was also Bart's job to operate the gramophone. He had to make sure he spun the wheel at a constant speed to the girls' pace.

The two girls started to dance a weird little hoochy-coochy dance,

from fragmented details of such performances found in books about the world referred to as the Eerie Exotic East. This involved undulating their bodies in suggestive ways to the beat of the music, and slowly removing their various veils. The audience assumed they were simply a pair of experienced dancers who had learnt how to move in unison. But as the music increased in tempo and those filmy, brightly-coloured pieces of cloth began to flutter to the ground, the two young ladies appeared, joined at the back.

Since their "creation", the girls had bloomed into two beautiful, shapely teenagers. Their silky brassieres were covered with beads and dangly tassels, and they wore semi-transparent silk genie pants. Little bells jingled around their wrists and ankles. The snakes protruding from their smooth bald heads moved as sinuously as medusa snakes, their tiny visages mimicking the expressions on the girls' own faces.

The audience had never seen such lovely girls, and there was quite a lot of lascivious leering and cat-calling. Sissy, who'd moved into the room after the last stragglers had paid their fees, pushed through the crowds to evict the rudest people. After all, these were her children, and no one was allowed to abuse them save her.

"This ain't that sorta show!" she growled as she booted the protesting lechers out into the darkness. "At least not 'til they're sixteen," she added under her breath.

Holly and Ivy were first and foremost belly-dancers, and Sissy had taught them well how to manoeuvre together. They'd been joined so seamlessly, and moved so perfectly, that the audience believed they were proper Siamese twins. Their dance may not have been accurate, but it had the desired effect. When the girls finished and flopped gracefully to the ground, pretending exhaustion, everyone clapped, cheered, and whooped. They jumped up and down and stomped their feet, shouting "More, more!"

"More will come, don't worry, my friends!" thundered Zak as the curtain closed. "Behold, the incredible Balloon Boy!"

The curtain parted with another flash and bang, and the mutant child known as Balloon Boy appeared, climbing up a ladder towards the tall point at the middle of the tent. At the top of the ladder was a diving board. Below, just the bare wooden stage. Currently the lad was wrapped in a cloak that hid his true form. At the top he straightened up.

"Oh, he's not, is he?"

Balloon Boy threw off his cloak to reveal his big round body and enormous mouth. He opened that mouth and jumped headfirst off the ledge. Suddenly his skin peeled away from around his face and body, puffing out like a parachute around him and allowing him to drop slowly and safely to the ground. He sprang onto his feet and bowed to thunderous applause.

"It's just a trick, a hoax," someone declared. "That's not skin, but a silk suit!"

The people enjoying the show by now far outweighed those who weren't, and each new freak drew more shouts and cries of amazement. "A genu-wine Jarboy rescued from one o' those vile Feratu Noi Body Snatchers ... Stilts ... Double-Decker Face ... the Gaggle Girls ..."

But Zak had left the best for last. "And now, my friends, a special treat." He eyed the audience coldly and calculatingly, casually twirling his cane in one hand. "You may have read books or seen pictures of a faraway world called Alkebula. But is it a mythical land, or is it real? Well, I'm here ta tell ya, without a shadow of a doubt, that it is *real*! It is a wondrous place full of strange and bizarre critters." The audience stared spellbound as Zak's hushed tones soared into a thunderous bellow. "Straight from the wilds of deepest, darkest Alkebula ... *preee-senting—Cheetah Boy*!"

Bart had saved his biggest smoke-bomb for his friend, and it went off with a spectacular report that caused more than one squeal of delight. On stage appeared Nathaniel, crouched as though to pounce, his ears pressed back against his skull, his catlike fangs bared in a vicious hiss. He was about to prance back and forth, necessitating Zak to "tame" him, when suddenly a woman in the audience shrieked, "*Nathaniel!*"

CHAPTER 20

After kicking out the perverts, Sissy remained outside the tent in the cool of the evening, making sure they didn't return. Then she started counting all the notes and coins in her purse. "Money! Wonderful money!" she cackled with glee. "We's got almost three hundred bucks here! That's a start! That's a *damn good* start! We don't even need any new supplies yet!" The fact that they'd already lost three of their exhibits didn't worry her. They could always make more.

Suddenly, from inside the tent came a cry of alarm, followed by a lot of shouting and commotion. Sissy sighed and rolled her eyes. "What's all the ruckus? Guess I'd better check it out!"

Stuffing the money back into her purse, she hitched up her voluminous skirts and marched back into the tent. She simply bulldozed through the concerned crowd to the source of the noise, and anyone who dared to block her way she straight-armed in the face, sending them to the floor. Sissy was getting stronger, but she didn't realise it.

She had always assumed she was that tough.

At the front of the tent, a tall, skinny blonde woman had managed to scramble up onto the stage, and was extending her arms towards Nate. Nate had backed up, and was on all fours with the fur around his neck and along his back raised, his tail quivering at attention, all teeth bared in a frightened hiss.

"Now see here, lady!" Zak reproved, brandishing his cane. "You can't just charge up on stage in the middle of a show! It's … it's just not proper!"

A stocky, curly haired man with a bushy beard was trying to pull the woman down, but despite his burly build he wasn't having much luck. "What're you doing, Louisa? You've gone wild!"

"That's my baby boy, Jake!" Louisa gestured towards Nate, who now appeared even more frightened and defensive. Bart, in his sparkly red leotard, emerged from behind the curtain to try and calm the cat-boy, who looked about to panic.

"No touching tha exhibits, ya crazy dame!" Zak shouted, slamming the base of his cane down on the stage with a loud thud. "Carn't you see how scared he is? Look at him!"

Sissy reached into the folds of her skirt, where she kept another pouch, a secret pouch, for emergencies. She'd anticipated the moment when something like this might be needed, but she'd always assumed she would be using it on one of her freaks, not a member of the audience.

Always knew this bitch would come back ta bite me on the behind one day, she thought darkly as she scrambled up on stage and grabbed Louisa by an arm. She drew her close as though to comfort her. "It's all right, dearie." Surreptitiously she jabbed her in the armpit with a needle. Louisa gasped in surprise. "We'll git to the bottom of this, don't you worry."

Still holding onto Louisa, Sissy turned, putting on a kindly, concerned face. "Are you her husband, sir?"

"Yes," said Jake.

"Wait," Louisa cried, but Sissy continued talking right over her. Her shrill tone was a lot louder.

"I think she may be a little hysterical, sir. We get a lotta folk becomin' agitated at our exhibits. 'Tis their confrontin' nature, you see. It's only natural. But don't you worry none. Jus' take her home, give 'er some tea an' put her ta bed, she'll be right as rain in the mornin'." With perfect timing, Sissy caught Louisa as she swooned.

Thinking this display was all part of the show, the audience gasped in amazement.

"Er, thank you," said Jake, looking a little overwhelmed.

Sissy carried Louisa off the stage in her arms, as though she weighed little more than a child, and handed her over to Jake. He took the unconscious Louisa from the tent to the mechanical horse he had parked outside. Meanwhile, Zak declared that the show was over, and the time had come for everyone to leave. Since almost two hours had passed, and the audience was more than satisfied, they were only too happy to start filing from the tent and heading home.

Sissy took Zak aside. "We need ta git packin' an' amscray right away!" she hissed at him.

Zak's eyes widened in surprise. "Surely not! No one'll believe that crazy bitch. Her story's far too absurd!"

"We don't wanna take no chances, Zak. Now git those lazy chillen *moving*!"

* * *

Jake took the woozy Louisa back to the Rancid Falls Hotel, where they were staying, and carried her up to their room, where he put her to bed. She tossed and mumbled as though delirious, and he became quite concerned. He thought she was having another Mescala worm flashback, but he'd never seen one so severe before. At least, not since he'd beaten down the door of her little room at the Rundowne Arms, and found her sweating and writhing on her bed. He fetched some tea as instructed and sat down beside her to comfort her, and eventually she fell into a deep slumber.

Jake began to regret not just taking the trackless train, but Louisa had insisted. She didn't want to set foot on that vile, filthy, dilapidated mode of transport ever again. If they were going to travel back to Mojo County, they'd do it on their own terms. So Jake had hired a mechanical horse, and they'd done the trip in stages. So far, so good, until now.

Jake was accompanying Louisa on her way back to Mojo Town to see her family for the first time since she'd left with Nathaniel. Her mother had sent a letter expressing reconciliation, but Louisa figured the old woman was merely after money upon learning that Louisa had married and obtained a Bhigge Smoche apartment. However, to give Mrs Bigelow the benefit of the doubt, Louisa had decided to see her. Rancid Falls was their very last stop before home.

Jake sighed and rubbed his eyes. Realising Louisa was out of the woods, he crawled in beside her and fell into his own deep, exhausted slumber.

Louisa woke, early the next morning, a little queasy but perfectly lucid. She remembered everything that had happened at the side-show—right up until that large woman came up on stage behind her and poked her in the armpit for some reason. That was when her senses had deserted her.

"You saw the cat-boy too, din't'choo?" she asked Jake.

"Ayuh."

"So you can't gainsay the mark on his face, the exact same mark that was on the face o' my poor little Nathaniel?" She pulled out the lumograph she carried with her everywhere and waved it in Jake's face.

It was a little battered and worse for wear, but she'd taken good care of it. Jake couldn't deny that mark. It was *exactly the same* as the mark that had been on that furry cheetah boy. Although the lumograph was sepia-toned, the baby boy in the picture had pale, pale eyes that, in real life, could have been the same blue as the cat-boy's—the same blue as Louisa's.

Jake sighed and waved Louisa's cigarette smoke out of his face. She always smoked when she was nervous.

"Was the lady who grabbed me very large, with curly grey hair, a pointy nose, dark eyes, and snaggleteeth?" Louisa asked.

"Yar," said Jake.

"That's the woman who runs the Mojo Town Orphanage." Louisa growled. "She told me Nate was dead and that she buried him. *I saw his grave.*"

"Louisa." Jake took her pale, trembling hands and squeezed them. "I believe you. I honestly do—I certainly saw enough last night. But that boy was at least ten years old."

Louisa stared at her kindly husband with a frightening intensity. "I don't know how he got older, but I'm sure some kind of supernatural trickery or experimental scientic skulduggery is at the root of it. After all, how did he git all catlike an' covered with fur, gawdammit?"

Jake had gone into that freak show with an open mind, and after seeing all those weird creatures, he was at a complete loss how to explain them. Were they really genuine freaks, or had some bizarre alchemic or scientic process been used to alter them? Being from Bhigge Smoche, he was used to seeing weird inventions, and doctors advertising in the paper for cadavers and volunteers to use to further their "revolutionary scientic advancements". He saw more than enough of their after-effects begging on the street, losing their hair or covered with suppurating sores and scabby skin. But none of them had been turned into genuine freaks like those children.

"Okay, Louisa. If you're well enough, let's go check the show out for sure before calling the sheriff."

*   *   *

The massive SandSub desert liner, the *SS Desert Devil*, had completed numerous trips through the desert since its maiden voyage a year earlier. It was so successful that its route had been changed to include not just Bhigge Smoche, but other large towns in the region. Not only could it cut through the smooth sand of the Mighty Desert like it was water, but also the rougher Scrubby Desert, where there were occasionally trees, grass, cacti, and bizarre lifeforms to provide more interesting obstacles.

Below the various desert sands lay hidden wonders: ancient ruins, vast underground lakes, and bizarre sand critters. The sub's thick portholes and glow-worm technology facilitated the viewing of these marvels while submerged.

Away from civilisation, small drones emerged from the SandSub to fly over the hills and dunes, looking out for hidden dangers. One scouted ahead, another hovered directly above, and a third followed behind. A new fandangled contraption unique to the SandSub liner, the drones were controlled by punch-card clockwork brains and held aloft by gyro blades. Each lasted an hour before their blades started to slow and they had to return to the sub to be wound back up. The sub carried a dozen replacement drones. Each was armed with state-of-the-art moon-crystal laser weaponry that enabled it to blast large rocks or anything that might be a threat to the SandSub, or potentially lodge in its giant rotating blades.

Whenever they approached a road, two of the drones landed on it to create a level crossing, warning other terrestrial vehicles that the SandSub was coming. Thus the sub was able to pass safely on through.

Previously, many steam-powered sandships and trackless trains that attempted to cross the Scrubby Desert were wrecked by the Perpetual Tornado. The Tornado's progress was erratic at the best of times, and impossible to predict because of its Vyking curse origins. Mostly zeppelins had the speed and agility to avoid it, but they were expensive and couldn't carry a lot of people or cargo.

Some wreckage of these old but magnificent craft could still be seen strewn around the desert, although most had been buried by the shifting sands. But the SandSub's unique structure allowed it to sink down under the sand to escape harm. Whenever the Perpetual Tornado was detected, hatches opened up on the sub, its drones stowed themselves inside their compartments, and then the hatches sealed behind them. The sub dived into the sand, leaving only its chimney and the very top of its periscope protruding, just enough to twist around and monitor the Tornado's progress. It had the capability to completely drop beneath the ground at the very last minute, if the Tornado passed directly overhead. Once the Tornado departed, the sub surfaced and the drones were released, so the massive contraption could continue its progress.

On this particular day the sub was travelling above the sand, but then the officer on lookout detected the Perpetual Tornado on direct approach. The drones were recalled and the sub slid beneath the surface, into emergency action mode. When the tornado passed, the sub resumed its journey.

The Perpetual Tornado swept up a lot of grit and tumbleweeds in its wake. Powerful gusts of wind sent large tangles of vegetation skidding along the sands and rolling down the massive dunes to slam into the sub's sides. Although passengers squealed and shrank back from the sight of these monstrous balls of foliage, the sub's reinforced steel hull was impervious to the flimsy weeds, and most disintegrated and were blown apart.

But then, as one of the "tumbleweeds" hit the side of the sub, it stuck there and unravelled, seeming to inflate to reveal a monstrous creature known as a *tumbleweed spider.* The creature moved by curling itself in a ball and rolling down the dunes, gathering weeds, sticks, and leaves in the process—a natural disguise to hide the true horror beneath.

Instead of spindly legs that would have made it difficult to move through the constantly shifting sands, the tumbleweed spider had eight long, sinuous tentacles festooned with fearsome claws that enabled it to cling to the machine's smooth sides. It had the furry black body and eight eyes of a spider, but the huge, beaky mouth of a squid. Multiple mandibles enabled it to punch holes in the sub's armour.

More tumbleweeds crashed into the sub, their vegetable coating blasting away to reveal more of these awful creatures. They unfurled to swarm the sub and start grappling with it. Passengers screamed at the sight of those massive segmented tentacles slamming across the windows, and the sound of the thick reinforced hull groaning and cracking beneath the pressure.

One tumbleweed spider blasted a sticky web over the windows of the control cabin, reducing visibility. Another managed to smash through a porthole and close its claws around a hapless crewman. That huge beaky mouth snapped closed around him and swallowed him whole.

The SandSub rocked and lurched as the tumbleweed spiders attacked. Pandemonium ensued as the passengers ran every which way, trying to find a safe haven.

At his control board, the SandSub commander released all the drones, and they immediately went into battle action. They blasted tentacles off some of the tumbleweed spiders that had managed to infiltrate the sub. One spider swiped at a drone with a tentacle, knocking it from the sky. The tiny flying machine spluttered and smashed against a rocky outcrop, exploding on impact.

The other drones continued to whiz around the SandSub, blasting the spiders with their lasers, singeing their bodies and tentacles. One scored a direct hit on a spider's eyes and fried its brain. It released its hold on the sub and flopped into the sand, dead.

One by one, the drones began to slow, and had to fly back to the SandSub for rewinding. The SandSub commander held his breath, hoping the rest would last for long enough. He'd never seen these tumbleweed spiders so numerous or so ferocious before. Then several drones, working together, managed to blast the abdomen off a second,

also knocking it from the sub. It shrieked and writhed in agony. A third spider, which had lost three tentacles, retreated from the machine. Two more drones managed to blow the head off a fourth.

By this stage, the spiders had had enough and began to retreat. A few had managed to grab human meals in the process, and their dead brethren would also serve to satisfy their prodigious appetites. Dragging their fallen comrades behind them, they drilled back down into the sand.

The remaining drones returned to be rewound and checked for damage.

The traumatised passengers watched the monsters sink down and disappear beneath the sand. Those in the rooms below decks saw them burrow past and vanish into the mysterious realms they occupied far below the surface.

Relieved, the SandSub commander flopped back into his chair. On this journey he'd seen more action than he cared for, and would be glad when they passed this section of desert and reached calmer sand.

As soon as the drones were ready to be re-released, the SandSub commander twisted several knobs on his control board, increasing the drones' aggression and reaction levels to maximum. This would reduce their flight time, but he didn't want to take any more chances, in case there were more terrors lurking out there.

CHAPTER 21

Louisa and Jake took their mechanical horse back to where the circus sideshow had been set up, but to their horror the site was bare, just churned-up dirt and grass left behind. There were a few broken pieces of wood, some old posters, a fire-pit, and a half-dug latrine, but nothing else.

"I don't believe it," Louisa moaned. "They's up and gone already!"

Jake prowled around, and then noticed some marks in the sand. "Look here, wheel tracks. The wind ain't covered 'em with sand yet, so it can't be too long since they left."

Louisa squinted. "Can you tell which way they went?"

"I think so."

"Can we catch up to them?"

"We'll give it a damn good go."

They scrambled back onto their hired mechanical horse, and Jake cranked it up as fast as it would go. Since it was only a horse carrying two people, not an articulated wagon-train loaded down with supplies, it could move almost as fast as the trackless train. A few hours later, the rear of Spindler's Sideshow caravan came into view. Badly-tied ropes fluttered in the wind, and some canvas had come loose from the roof and was flapping madly.

"There they are!" Louisa cried excitedly.

At the front of the wagon, Zak hung onto the reins with Bart beside him, making a record of everything that had happened the night before. He was wondering if there was any way he could get in contact with Nate's mother.

Suddenly Sissy poked her head out of her window. The wind tore at her curly grey hair. "Move it, Zak! We're being followed!" she shouted.

"What?" Zak rose in his seat and peered around the side of the wagon. He could see the small mechanical horse fast approaching, a large cloud of dust behind it.

Zak tugged on the reins, but he'd already pulled them back as far as they could go. "I cain't go no faster, Sissy! We's loaded to tha hilt. This is the wagon's top speed!"

Inside the wagon, Sissy hauled herself out of her cabin and pushed her way down the centre aisle, through the tightly-packed luggage and seated children, towards the doors at the back. She flung the doors wide with a clatter.

"This'll slow 'em up an' lighten tha load!" she shouted, and grabbed the first thing within reach. With her superior strength, she flung the object from the wagon, and it hurtled towards the horse.

"Look out, Jake!" Louisa shrieked. "Something's being thrown from the back of the wagon!"

Balloon Boy opened his mouth as he flew, sucking in air to try and slow his mad velocity, but he couldn't control his flight, and slammed into the front of their mechanical horse. With a howl of despair, he fell under the heavy metal wheels with a sickening crunch.

Louisa screamed, and Jake cursed as he tried to control the vehicle.

But Balloon Boy's loose skin became twisted and tangled around the disk wheels, preventing them from gaining traction on the road. Jake knew if he hit the brakes now, they'd flip over, so he tried to slow by turning, and they veered off into the scrub. Balloon Boy's skin tore and he came loose from the vehicle, sliding into a tangled, bloody mess in the middle of the road.

*　*　*

At the sight of Sissy so casually sacrificing one of them to try and stop that horse, the other children started to scream and cry.

"Stop that infernal racket, you stupid brats!" Sissy shouted at them, all reason lost. She could feel something shifting beneath her clothing, and realised that the growths Bart had removed had returned after only a few days. The Stuff in her system had finally reached saturation point and was starting to react. The angrier she got, the more it bubbled in her bloodstream, causing her cells to shift and mutate.

"What's goin' on down there?" Zak yelled from the driver's seat. When he didn't receive an answer, he turned to Bart. "Git down there an' find out what's goin' on!"

Bart twisted in his seat, opening a small wooden panel behind him. He slid down into the little cabin Sissy and Zak shared, crawled across their beds, and pushed the inner door open to pandemonium.

All the children were out of their seats now. Some were simply screaming hysterically. Others were trying to get their windows open so they could escape. Nate was meowing in terror, and Anna was curled around a beam, hissing and snarling. The children's frantic motion was causing the vehicle to start sliding from one side of the road to the other.

"Shut up an' siddown, you obnoxious shits!" Sissy bellowed from the back of the vehicle. Even from his vantage point, Bart could see that there was something wrong with her. Her face was bulging with tumorous growths, and beneath her long, shapeless dress, her body was shifting and bulging. Then the flowered cloth started to rip.

Bart darted back into the little cabin and scrambled out through the hatch. Other kids spotted his retreat and started to follow.

"You gotta slow down!" Bart shouted as he climbed back onto his seat.

"Quit buggin' me, brat! I know what I'm doin'!" Zak shouted as he hung onto the control lever.

Bart tried to grab the lever to take over, but Zak cuffed him across the temple, knocking him from his seat. He nearly fell from the vehicle, but managed to catch onto the railing at the last second. A pretty face emerged from the hatch. It belonged to Anna. "What's going on here?" she wanted to know.

The control lever wrenched in Zak's hands, and he lost control of the vehicle. It started to fishtail across the sandy road.

* * *

The SandSub flowed serenely through the desert on its journey. It hadn't run into any further trouble since the battle with the tumbleweed spiders, and was on course towards Bhigge Smoche. As it approached the path used by the trackless train, several drones hovered about, scanning for danger. Two of the drones settled on the road, creating a level-crossing. They started to emit a high-pitched whine of warning while arming their weaponry.

* * *

Zak struggled to regain control of the wagon. "You gotta slow down, Uncle Zak!" Anna cried, trying to curl around the lever herself. Bart, still clinging to the railing of his seat, kicked and struggled to clamber back in, but the machine's wild gyrations made that nearly impossible.

"These kids are outta control, Sissy!" he shouted.

"*Sit down! All of you! Stop that crying!*" Sissy roared from inside the wagon. Her growths extended, twisted and enlarged. They tore through her dress, and the cloth came away from her body. But the horrific sight of her only made the children more upset, and the bedlam increased as the youngsters hurled themselves at the windows. One or two broke open, and the kids tried to scramble out. But they were too scared to drop and tumble onto the road below.

"*SHUT UP! SHUT UP! SHUT UP!*"

* * *

A flash of light caught Zak's peripheral vision, snapping his attention forward. Too late, Zak noticed the level crossing with the SandSub passing through directly in front of him. Because the sand here was coarse and rocky, dotted with the occasional stunted tree, the SandSub was travelling partly above the surface. Its periscope and control room were visible above the sand, with the rest beneath.

The SandSub was so large and heavily fortified that it probably wouldn't incur a scratch if crashed into, but the drones were programmed not to take any chances. As the out-of-control wagon train approached, the closest drone activated. Still set at the heightened aggression level, it blasted the wagon with its laser.

The boiler ruptured and exploded, sending the wagon tumbling sideways. It rolled over and over across the sand and grass, wheels flying off, windows smashing, wooden panels shattering and crumbling. Flames from the engine engulfed the driver's seat and the front portion of the wagon, hungrily consuming its wooden and flammable parts.

Finally it slid to a stop, a mess of twisted metal and broken bodies.

The SandSub continued on its way, oblivious to the carnage on the road. The two drones acting as a level crossing activated their gyro copters, picked themselves up, and returned to their monitoring positions around the machine.

* * *

Louisa and Jake hurried over to Balloon Boy to see if they could do anything for him, but their mechanical horse had torn his loose skin to shreds and shattered his bones. He lay in a crumpled, mangled heap, his eyes staring lifelessly from his shattered skull.

"Dad-zizzle, we nearly crashed!" Jake exclaimed. "We can't do anythin' for this poor lad, but are you all right?"

"Yar, fine, fine. But we've gotta get Nathaniel, Jake. We've got to." Louisa clutched his arms, squeezing them emphatically.

"All right." Jake checked the mechanical horse for damage. It had sustained some dents and scratches, and he had to pull some of Balloon Boy's torn skin from the gears, but it still appeared to be running. He helped Louisa aboard and they continued down the road, towards a plume of smoke rising into the sky.

As they came roaring over a hill, the source of the pollution was revealed. The articulated wagon had crashed, and the front was on fire. Dead bodies were strewn all over the road.

Louisa screamed.

"What the hell's happened here?!" Jake gasped in horror.

Louisa sprang down from the horse before it had even finished moving, and raced over to the bodies. "Nate, Nate," she sobbed as she checked each one. "Please be all right, my boy, please. I don't care that you're a cat now. *Please.*"

But when they found Nathaniel's body, it was twisted and bloody. He'd been thrown from the wagon as it was rolling and tumbling, and his spine had shattered in the process. Jake checked him over and then carefully picked up his limp, broken body, cradling it in his arms.

"I'm afraid he's dead, Louisa," he said softly.

Louisa hung her head over him and burst into tears. "My poor little wine-stained boy…"

Jake carried Nate over to their mechanical horse and tucked him into the storage compartment on the back. "We'll take him back into town … give him a proper burial there. But first we gotta look for survivors."

Cautiously, Jake and Louisa approached the wreckage once more. The front was still burning, but they realised that when the flames reached the back, the whole thing would go up like a firecracker. Oil from a ruptured canister had formed a large puddle near the shattered back doors.

"Hello?" Jake called. "Is anyone inside? We're here to help."

* * *

Sissy lay on the ground in a heap in front of the burning wreckage. Acrid smoke billowed across the sky. She sluggishly opened her eyes. A fuzzy abstract of twisted metal and carnage surrounded her.

When she finally focussed, she noticed her dear brother still sitting in the driver's seat, although the seat was detached from the wagon. He lay slumped over the detached steering column, which was protruding out his back, impaling him.

Anger surged within her. All their dreams, all their hopes, dashed, dead.

The Stuff coursed through her veins, distorting her. Turning her rage into flesh.

She arose from the wreckage as a monster.

* * *

From behind the wreckage, a large shape swelled, and a giant hand reached out towards Jake. Festering with brilliant green boils and tumorous growths of all shapes and sizes, fingers ending in murderous talons, the hand curled around Jake and lifted him high into the air.

Sissy Spindler rose from the smashed wagon to many feet into the air, now mutated into a horrific mountain of flesh: gnarly, warty growths; tentacles; multiple limbs; and a giant slobbering mouth crammed with sharp and misshapen teeth. With a thunderous roar, she took the hapless Jake in her numerous limbs and ripped him apart, throwing his portions in all directions.

"Ya meddlin' bitch! Couldn't leave well enough alone!" Sissy roared, her voice now so loud and deep it shook through the ground.

Louisa screamed.

"Ya kilt me poor brother an' all our dreams! Now I'm gonna crush you!"

Another of Sissy's giant hands reached down to grab Louisa. She turned and ran.

"Yer cain't escape me, girlie! Aha ha ha!" Sissy roared.

Louisa yanked out her flint lighter and hurled it onto the spilt oil. "Burn, you bitch!" She shrieked as the giant, clawed fingers reached for her. She ducked and flung herself sideways.

Suddenly the spilt oil caught fire. Immediately gigantic flames shot up, billowing around Sissy's monstrous body. She bellowed in agony, slapping at the flames with her many limbs, but she only succeeded in spreading the oil and fire further. She tried to haul her massive form from the flames, but her mutation had accelerated to such a degree that her legs had fused, and she was now sessile. She tumbled forward, crashing into the wreckage, where the flames quickly consumed her.

Her dying thoughts were of the water-globe with the decorative house inside. She had often dreamt of living in that fairy-tale house with a loving husband and a large family. The water-globe had encapsulated and symbolised all her dreams. But throughout her life, her dreams had been unattainable, becoming distorted and twisted...

And as the acrid black smoke invaded her throat and started to choke

her lungs, she managed to croak out one last word. "...Rosewell..."

* * *

Louisa stumbled from the flaming wreckage, coughing, spluttering, and trying not to be sick. That horrific creature and what it had done would forever haunt her thoughts. But as she was heading back to the mechanical horse and Nate's body, she heard a soft groan.

Louisa turned, noticing a body slung over the low-lying branch of a nearby tree. Had someone actually survived this horror? She hurried over to the body and carefully pulled down the semi-conscious form of a perfectly ordinary boy with curly brown hair. He had torn clothes and a smoke-blackened face, but he appeared to be all right. He blinked and focussed on Louisa's face.

"H-hello," he said softly. "Did you save me?"

"I found you in that tree." Louisa pointed it out.

Bart blinked at it. The last thing he remembered was the engine exploding in front of him. How on Earth had he ended up in a tree? Then he noticed some marks in the sand around the roots. They looked like the tracks of a snake, and they disappeared off into the scrub.

Had *Anna* saved him?

Louisa helped him up. He stood on shaky legs. "Is ... is anyone else alive?" he asked. "Nate?"

Sadly, Louisa shook her head. "You're the last..." She tailed off, realising that she didn't know his name.

He held out a grubby hand. "I'm Barton."

"Louisa Bigelow." They shook hands. "Come on. I'll take you back to town. The sheriff'll need to be contacted 'bout this."

* * *

Since Louisa had lost both her husband and son, and didn't have anyone else, she adopted Bart, and he took her surname as his own. She received a small inheritance from Jake and used it to send Bart to school, for not long after they met, she discovered just how brilliant he was. She wanted him to go far in life, and indeed he did. He received a scholarship to attend the prestigious Academy of Medicine in Bhigge Smoche, where he excelled. He graduated a full doctor early and started his own practise, but soon discovered that a life of lancing boils on rich snobs' backsides and sewing up their spoilt children's split heads wasn't for him.

After his experiences with the Spindlers' Sideshow, he decided to build a decent home for society's freaks and unfortunates. He created his own sideshow circus, one that was founded on respect rather than fear; all performers would be well-housed and paid for their services, rather than bullied and beaten.

* * *

Dr Barton Bigelow straightened up from the graves of Louisa, Jake, and Nathaniel. He came here regularly to visit them and pay his respects, but he had dallied here long enough.

He lifted a gloved hand to his hat and removed it, holding it against his chest in quiet contemplation. His once thick curls had receded, forming a fringe around the back of his head. Previously, those unruly locks had effectively concealed the other side effect of what the Stuff had done to him, the one that Sissy had never noticed.

As the Stuff had enhanced his intelligence so significantly, his brain had grown larger than normal. This had caused his head to grow bigger as well. Now, without hair to cover it, his forehead was highly domed.

"Goodbye," he told the graves. "I shall be back to visit you again soon." He put his tall crimson top hat back on to conceal his domed head and heightened intelligence. He returned to his circus.

The show must go on...

* * *

A beautiful young woman stood on the sweeping veranda of a large stately home. A handsome young army officer with an impressive waxed moustache climbed the front steps towards her.

Children of varying ages rushed past him and into the house, shrieking and laughing with excitement.

The officer took the woman into his arms and kissed her lovingly. Then they stepped inside and closed the front door just as flakes of grey ash began to fall.

The sign beside the door read: "Rosewell".

Carter Rydyr (a.k.a. SCAR) are:
Antoinette Rydyr—Original Concept and
Writer
Steve Carter—Writer and Illustrator

The strange and bizarre works by SCAR incorporates anything from sci-fi and horror fantasy, to surrealism and weird satire. All of it has a strong element of the fantastic and a healthy dose of experimentalism. They create in a variety of mediums—prose fiction, illustration, comic books, screenplays, and even music with their experimental bands FistFunk Futurists and TeknoSadisT, which can be sampled on Bandcamp at teknosadist.bandcamp.com.

Their fiction stories have appeared in "Surreal Worlds" and "More Bizarro Than Bizarro" published by Bizarro Pulp Press; "Aliens, Sex & Sociopaths: The Best of Surreal Grotesque" and Antipodean SF.

In 2010, their original screenplay, *Curse of the Swampies*, a horror sci-fi film, won Best Feature Film Screenplay at the A Night of Horror International Film Festival.

Their controversial comic book trilogy, *Spore Whores*, is currently being reprinted by Bloody Gore Comix in Canada, and they have recently published several graphic novels, including *Savage Bitch*, *Weird Worlds: Subversive Science Fiction Stories*, *Bestiary of Monstruum*, *Weird Sex Fantasy: Tales of Sex and Death for the Totally Jaded*, *Fantastique*, and *Phantastique: Tales of Taboo Terror*, which celebrates the resurrection of the controversial *Phantastique*, ingloriously presented in full bloody colour!

More grotesque delights can be viewed on their website: weirdwildart.com or visit their Amazon Author Page.

Ethan Somerville—Writer

Ethan Somerville is a prolific Australian author with over 70 books published in numerous genres. He has authored the *Eridon Chronicles, the Curse of the Kingsmans, the Circus Infinitus, Mirrorworld, Mission, American Psychics* and the popular, long-running *Nocturnal Academy* series. He recently collaborated with fellow Australian author Carter Rydyr to create the steampunk western *Weird Wild West*, parts one and two now published by Bizarro Pulp Press. He has also collaborated with other Australian writers and artists, including Max Kenny, Emma Daniels, Anthony Newton, Colin Forest and Tanya Nicholls.

Visit the website: www.stormpublishing.net

Visit Ethan's facebook page at www.facebook.com/Ethan.Somerville.writer

www.ingramcontent.com/pod-product-compliance
Lightning Source LLC
Chambersburg PA
CBHW020953180626
46814CB00003B/1076